MAYBE WE'RE ELECTRIC

ALSO BY
VAL EMMICH

Dear Evan Hansen: The Novel

The Reminders

MAYBE WE'RE ELECTRIC

VAL EMMICH

POPPY
LITTLE, BROWN AND COMPANY
New York Boston

Poppy
Hachette Book Group
1290 Avenue of the Americas, New York, NY 10104
Visit us at LBYR.com

First Edition: September 2021

Poppy is an imprint of Little, Brown and Company.
The Poppy name and logo are trademarks of Hachette Book Group, Inc.

The publisher is not responsible for websites (or their content)
that are not owned by the publisher.

Library of Congress Cataloging-in-Publication Data
Names: Emmich, Val, author.
Title: Maybe we're electric / Val Emmich.
Other titles: Maybe we are electric
Description: First edition. | New York : Little, Brown and Company, 2021. | "Poppy." | Audience: Ages 14 & up. | Summary: In Edison, New Jersey, in a museum devoted to the inventor Thomas Edison, a loner sixteen-year-old girl with a limb difference and the seemingly coolest boy in school spend the night during a snowstorm, growing close until a shameful secret threatens everything.
Identifiers: LCCN 2020043348 | ISBN 9780316535700 (hardcover) | ISBN 9780316535694 (ebook) | ISBN 9780316499132 (ebook other)
Subjects: CYAC: Self-acceptance—Fiction. | People with disabilities—Fiction. | Secrets—Fiction.
Classification: LCC PZ7.1.E475 May 2021 | DDC [Fic]—dc23
LC record available at https://lccn.loc.gov/2020043348

ISBNs: 978-0-316-53570-0 (hardcover), 978-0-316-53569-4 (ebook)

Printed in the United States of America

LSC-C

Printing 1, 2021

You are seeing what nobody else
ever witnessed before tonight or
outside of this room.

—Thomas Edison

You don't want to be a monster. Not anymore. You don't want to feel ugly. Inside or out.

Thomas Edison said that failure is guaranteed. The part that matters is what you do after. You used to doubt this, but now you believe. Which is why you're going back to retrace your steps. Maybe there's still a way to fix the damage you've done. To face the ugly and make a more beautiful after.

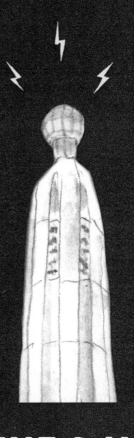

THE DAY
OF THE STORM

I 'm huddled on the hard floor of the museum, back pressed to a slow-warming baseboard, waiting for the shivering to stop.

The checkered floor beneath me is cracked in places, and this cracks me in places, the reminder that everything begins new and near perfect but eventually cracks in places.

Around me are a hundred faces, each in black and white, most belonging to the man of honor, the inventor who once turned this unremarkable spot in New Jersey into a world-wide destination and later had the whole town named after him.

Along with these photos of Thomas Edison are working models of his many inventions. Incandescent bulbs. Sound devices. Telephone transmitters. A dozen of the four hundred patents developed in Menlo Park cover the wall. Inside a glass tank is a model of the laboratory that once stood on these grounds. It's all crammed into a space no bigger than my living room.

But it's better than my living room. I don't want to be anywhere near home right now. I just wish I had grabbed a few essentials before storming out of the house earlier. Mainly my phone. A jacket, too, would have been smart.

I compose an email in my head to my dad: *She's the worst. I mean it. She ruined everything. Please don't take her side right now. I don't need that.* I can imagine his reply: *Mom's doing her best. Not taking her side, I promise. Yes, she can be the worst. We all can be.*

I hug my knees and drop my wet face into the abyss I've made in between. I shake quietly—for a minute, an hour.

I'm startled by a familiar beep. Everyone who works here knows that annoying beep. It yanks our attention away from whatever we're doing and alerts us that someone has entered the museum.

I forgot to lock the door behind me.

Maybe Mom chased after me in the snow. It can't be Charlie; he already left for his gig and missed the drama at home. If it is Mom, she's got me cornered. The Thomas Edison Center possesses a lot of things, but space isn't one of them. There's the front room, back room (where I am now), bathroom, and tiny utility closet. A back door leads outside, to a shed and the memorial tower, but opening it will sound another beep.

"Hello?" says a voice that definitely isn't my mom's.

I keep still, hoping the voice and whomever it belongs to will leave as quickly as they came.

A shadow spreads down the hall and into the back room.

It stops, and I lift my eyes. A hooded figure looms above. Snow sheds onto the floor as the hood comes off.

I know him. He's in my grade, a fellow sophomore. His name is Mac Durant. Mac Durant, as in list whatever desirable attribute you can think of—gorgeous, bright, charming, popular, star athlete, too-good-to-be-true heartthrob cliché from every teenage rom-com you've ever seen—with the absurdly appropriate name to go with it, Mac Durant. What the hell is *he* doing here?

I'm a hot mess. I'm two-day-old hair. I'm a ratty sweatshirt. I'm worn-out leggings and mismatched socks. It's not like I'm super thrilled with my presentation even on full-effort days, when I'm actually *expecting* to be seen, but this look I've got going on right now, complete with puffy red eyes, is next-level tragic.

I wipe my face with my sleeve and do my best impersonation of a stable person. His giant golden eyes stare in confusion. He's probably trying to remember my name. Who is this girl I pass by daily but with whom I never interact? And why is she curled up in a shaky ball on this dirty cracked floor?

"I need your phone," Mac Durant says. "It's an emergency."

These are not the words I prepared for, or the voice I imagined delivering them. Hearing distress in a person who only ever oozes confidence rattles me even more.

The museum is closed, I want to say. He's not supposed to be here, and neither am I.

"Please," Mac says, polite but desperate.

My right hand rises and my finger points. He turns in a hurry, his shadow trailing. I get up and step into the hallway, a spy at the corner. He reaches for the old phone, but he doesn't lift the receiver. That's when I notice the blood on his hand.

He looks up and sees me.

"You do it," he says.

I struggle to speak.

He lifts the receiver. "I need you to make the call. I'll tell you what to say."

His eyes show no malice, only urgency.

I watch his bloody hand press three numbers. Any call that can be made with just three numbers is a call I want no part of.

I'm about to advise him of this new and unwritten policy of mine, but he beckons me with rapid waving and the use of my name. "Tegan," he says. His saying my name, knowing my name—it's too much.

I let him pass me the receiver.

A faint voice: "911. What's your emergency?"

Mac gestures for me to lift the receiver to my ear. It's like he has to teach me how to use a device I've never seen before, as if I'm back in Edison's time. This is what a person does when making a call on a telephone. She places the top of the receiver to her ear and the bottom to her mouth and she speaks.

But what does she say?

"I'd like to report something," Mac whispers, instructing me what to tell the dispatcher.

I can't. I'm mute. He implores me with his giant stare, and sure enough I hear myself repeat his words verbatim: "I'd like to report something."

Mac squints achingly before giving me my next line. "There's a man inside a garage."

"There's a man..." I say.

"Inside a garage," Mac says.

"Inside a garage."

"His car is running. Inside the garage."

"His car is running inside the garage," I repeat.

"I think he might be trying to hurt himself," Mac says.

I pause. Mac nods. It's okay. All of this is okay. His eyes promise me: *We're in this together.*

I tell the dispatcher, "He might be trying to hurt himself."

Mac gives me two thumbs up. I hold the receiver away from my mouth and tell Mac that the dispatcher wants an address.

"Eighty-eight Anchorage Road," Mac says.

I give the address to the dispatcher, and only afterward does the information register. Mac lives on Anchorage, walking distance from here, the opposite direction from where I live. The museum is roughly midway between our houses.

The dispatcher asks for my name. Mac hears this and mouths for me to hang up. I hesitate. He takes the receiver and hangs up for me.

The museum is silent, still.

I notice his bloody hand on the receiver. He shoves it into his coat pocket.

Mac Durant takes a deep breath, his shoulders lifting, and

exhales. All the tension he entered the museum with fades away. A transformation. He's the guy I've always observed, trouble-free dimple, gooey golden eyes, swagger for days, and he's staring at me, *me*, saying the most straightforward word in the most non-straightforward of situations:

"Thanks."

The phone lies quiet between us. We stare at it like it's a body dumped in a dirt hole. I wrestle with the realization that I've just participated in something major and I have no idea what it is.

Mac begins to explain. "It was weird. I was walking and I see this guy. He's sitting in his car, in his garage."

I wait for the rest of the story, but he just smiles, as if to say, *Well, that was fun. What should we do next?*

Hold on. After what he made me do, he owes me a proper explanation. He was walking *where*? In a *snowstorm*? What made him think the guy was trying to hurt himself? Wouldn't the garage door need to be closed? Then how did Mac see him? Also, if he was so close to home, on his own street, why didn't he call from his house? And, oh yeah, what happened to his hand?

Too bad I can't say any of this out loud. It doesn't work like that. Talking here means bending the laws of our shared universe in which he imposes his will and I silently obey.

My wonder only worsens when Mac reaches into his coat

pocket and lights up his phone. His *phone!* The one he could have used to call for help *on his own.*

I can't let this slide. Universe be damned. "Cool phone," I blurt out.

He examines the phone, searching for what's so cool about it. "Thanks," he says, looking at me like *I'm* the weird one here.

He pockets the phone and scans the room. "I've never actually been inside this place. I walk by it all the time but..."

He's on the move now, a dashing figure even in crisis: baggy chinos, white trainers, and a puffy winter coat with a faux-fur hood. He approaches the Thomas Edison bust that greets all visitors when they enter the museum. The Wizard of Menlo Park, they call him. Edison, not Mac Durant. Although, honestly, the name works for both.

"So this is him," Mac says, casual as can be. "The man. The myth. The legend."

"The myth," I say, my own voice surprising me.

Mac shows off his deep dimple. "Not a fan?"

I shrug. Like my dad, I was fond of Thomas Edison once, but now I find him pretty overrated.

Anyway, what are we even talking about? Why is Mac smiling as if he finds this amusing? I'm simultaneously shaken with fear over the unfamiliar gravity of the situation and put off by the gross predictability of it. Am I in serious danger or simply trapped in the same tireless high school reality show I live through daily? Because in a way it's so typical for a guy like Mac Durant to barge in here as if he owns the joint, every door on god's playground swinging open for him, every girl he deems worthy of his golden gaze doing his random bidding, even becoming his accomplice in possibly criminal acts. And what now? We're just hanging out having an innocent chat?

My eyes fall to the floor. Added to the checkered pattern are new imperfections: red dots. I trace the trajectory up to Mac's hand, which was just touching the Edison bust.

"No," I say.

"What's up?"

"No, no, no."

"Are you okay?"

I point: Thomas Edison has a bloody nose.

"Shit," Mac says. "My bad."

I rush off and return with paper towels and cleaning spray. I wipe the floor and tend to Mr. Edison while Mac tries to plug up his rude wound. He does a bad job of it.

I retrieve the first-aid kit from behind the front counter. I've seen it used only once (for a bee sting). Judging from the yellowed Band-Aids, the kit may predate the artifacts it shares space with.

I place the kit on the counter, open the lid, and give a dramatic sigh. "Come here," I say.

Mac brings his hand over to the glass display counter. The display holds Thomas Edison merchandise. Light bulb key chains. Light bulb stress balls. Light bulb notepads. Light bulb light bulbs. Genius Water sells for one dollar—a steal. An Edison bobblehead stands on the case. Mac gives it a poke and the head nods *yes, yes, yes, yes, yes.*

I gesture to Mac's hand. He seems unsure. Again, it's hard

to fathom what I'm seeing: The guy who seems always to float while the rest of us walk two-footed is grounded. Not grounded as in steady. Grounded as in unable to freely fly.

I know the feeling better than anyone; there's nothing more vulnerable than showing your hand.

"Normally I'd let you bleed as much as you want," I say. "But right now isn't a good time for me."

He grins. It's a smile to break atoms.

He uncurls his fist and places his hand flat on the counter.

I use my own hands, both of them, to reach into the kit and grab supplies. Bandage, scissors, cream. First, alcohol. I dab a cotton ball and press the soaked side to Mac's skin. He winces.

"This will sting a little," I tell him.

"I think you're supposed to say that *before* you do it."

Fair enough.

I dab at his pink-and-purple bruise, his raw inside. Reality seeps in. The thought of what I'm doing and with whom. How's my breath? My hair? My eyebrows? Not that it matters. When people look at me, their focus is usually elsewhere. On the counter are four hands, and one is clearly not like the others. My left hand has only two fingers. I guarantee Mac is staring at it. To test my theory, I drag my left hand away from the action and track Mac's eyes to see whether they follow. They do.

I pull my hand away, and he catches himself, tries to act natural. At least he doesn't apologize. That's the worst— when people apologize as if they've just walked in on you naked and seen a part of you that's meant to be hidden away.

I grab a tube of cream. "Rub this on yourself," I say, realizing too late how that sounded. I squeeze, and the tube farts out cream onto his unharmed hand. Not awkward at all. Now I'm the one trying to act natural. "Have fun," I say.

He laughs softly and applies the cream to his wound. It spreads into a thin, transparent glisten, his skin slippery. He covers the tender area, fingers gently massaging. This should be happening in private, whatever this is.

Mac lifts his hand to his nose and sniffs. He throws his hand at me. "Smell this."

"No," I say, leaning away.

"Can this stuff go bad?"

I inspect the hard-crinkled tube. "It expired in 2003."

He takes another whiff and recoils.

Curiosity overtakes me. "Fine, let me smell."

He presents his hand. There's definitely a scent. He's not imagining it. I sniff the tube to see if it's a match, but the cream barely has a smell.

"I think it's you," I say. "It's your blood."

"What do you mean, my blood?"

"You have bad blood."

"My blood is not bad," he says confidently.

"I mean, from like, whatever happened."

He looks down at his hand, his atomic smile disarmed. I must have said the wrong thing. Meanwhile his poor wound lies there undressed.

"We should cover it," I say.

I begin to wrap his wound with a bandage. It means pulling out my left hand. Returning it to the table.

As I bandage him, round and round, my old frustration returns. I have questions and he has answers, and instead of coming out and asking my questions, I keep going round and round in cowardly ignorance.

The chance to break the cycle may never come again.

I ask my question: "What happened?"

He shuts his eyes.

Let me guess. Chopping wood for a fire. Saving a cat from a tree. Volunteer snow shoveling.

"I smashed a brick," Mac says, stripping the violence from what seems like a violent act, as if what he did was the only thing that could have been done.

I try to picture it, the smashing of the brick, and Mac doing it, but it's a video that never loads. I can't see it happening—this unflappable person losing his cool.

What I do see is how Mac feels about what happened: a muddled mix of shame and remorse and something like pride.

He opens his eyes and waits for my reaction.

"Well," I say, after thinking it through. "Your hand still looks better than mine."

I smile at my joke, so he can feel safe to do the same.

You were born different. The rest of the babies are given ten fingers and ten toes. Not you. You get one hand with only two fingers—thumb and ring—and barely those two. The condition is known as symbrachydactyly. It's a word that hurts your brain to look at. Someone very creative invented a simpler name for it. When a person has limbs that look different, they are said to have, drumroll please, *limb difference*. Your parents go their own way. They call your left hand your *special* hand.

Early on, your parents give serious consideration to surgery, but in the end, opt against it. They instead place all their hope in a risky approach called self-acceptance. At first, it seems to work. You are a carefree and oblivious child. You don't know what it's like to have ten fingers. Nothing feels amiss. Mom and Dad let you figure things out on your own. Buttoning shirts is annoying, and you never feel like you have a solid grip on your bike's handlebars. But this stuff isn't odd. It just is.

Then you get older. You notice people staring. They've always stared, but you really sense it now. Your best friend since kindergarten, Isla, defends you fiercely against giggling boys. You begin to see yourself anew. For the first time, a doctor describes you as having a "disability." You always knew you were different, but this new term—despite how matter-of-factly it's delivered—makes it seem as if something's wrong with you. Doubt creeps in about how "normal" you really are. You start to obsess about your difference in a way you know is unhealthy and unhelpful. You stare at your hand until it isn't a hand anymore. It's a mini calzone strapped to your wrist. Or a snake that swallowed an old TV antenna. It's the last piece of tape salvaged from a roll that gets stuck to itself and becomes a frustrated tangle.

You try to draw people's attention away from the thing that makes you different. You wear long sleeves in summer. Shirts with bold, distracting slogans on the front. You make jokes, lots, most at your own expense.

When you hit your teens, you're over it. You're bored of the subject. Really, who cares? It's just a hand. Nothing *special*, far from it. No one pays attention to a hand. Not you. Not your family or friends. You're all aware of it, but you don't focus on it. Only strangers seem to care. The problem is there are many strangers, always more coming, reminding you of what you keep forgetting. It's exhausting. You don't have the energy to educate every new person you meet. Or to battle the old people in your life who still don't know better. It's easier just to sink into the background. To avoid their eyes. To make yourself small. To make yourself very, very quiet.

I refill the first-aid kit and return the box to a bottom shelf. I stay low behind the counter, fiddling for longer than is realistic. I need a chance to think.

What was that phone call about? Why ask *me* to place the call? And the blood! We can't forget the bad blood!

Maybe I'll stand up and Mac will have magically disappeared and I can go back to worrying about just me.

I rise and my prayer is answered. He's gone.

That was easy.

I peer out the window. No sign of him. I scurry to the front door and crank the sticky lock, shutting out the world. My sigh is the sound of relief.

Or is it disappointment? Did the most exciting moment of my life just pass me by? He was here a second ago, I swear: Mac Durant. He left without saying goodbye. Or thanking me for bandaging his hand.

A sound from the back room turns me around. When I get there, Mac is handling one of the phonographs.

"Careful," I say, relieved to find him still here and yet

frightened all over again. He's scary in the way a unicorn would be if you met one: You just assumed the thing wasn't real.

I step in and catch the tonearm before it touches the disc. We've already soiled Mr. Edison's face. The last thing I need is to be responsible for damaging one of these priceless machines.

"This is from the thirties," I say. "It's irreplaceable."

"We've got a turntable at home."

"Not like this one."

"Pretty similar."

It's nice, I guess, that his confidence is back in full force, but unfortunately he has no idea what he's talking about.

"Does it work?" Mac says.

Even in his current state—oily hair pointing everywhere, cheeks a very relatable red—Mac wields a power that's hard to defend against.

Yes, the turntable works. It can't play any odd record, only Edison's proprietary discs, and those strictly on the guided tours. The museum is open four days a week. Today, Saturday, it closed at four and will reopen tomorrow at ten, weather permitting. But I haven't worked at the Thomas Edison Center in months, and neither of us should be here right now.

Except we are.

Fine. Quickly.

I swing open the front panel of our largest phonograph and drop the stylus. The music is egregiously peppy. We listen for a long minute (not easy). I feel unjustly responsible for what we're listening to, as if I'm the artist who recorded the song and Mac's assessment of it reflects on me personally. His foot appreciates the beat, tapping a nimble rhythm. He peeks at his phone and tucks it away. When the music finally ends, I holster the stylus and shut the panel.

"It's a huge hit with the over-ninety crowd," I say, hoping to distance myself from the snoozefest he was forced to endure.

He moves to another exhibit. His stroll—leisurely, inquisitive—creates the absurd impression that this was his plan all along for this Saturday night, to brush up on his long-ignored Thomas Edison history. I follow his movements, studying his profile (for security purposes, of course). His nose is pronounced and it works for him. His lips appear painted on with an expensive brush; to be honest, I've had daydreams about smearing his paint.

"Shouldn't you be closing?" Mac says. "It's looking bad out there."

He gives me a once-over, absorbing my appearance only now, every curious inch of it. The laundry-shrunk red sweatshirt I've been loafing around in all day is my go-to for comfort and laziness, but it makes for unconvincing work attire. I may sound like an official employee of the museum, but I definitely don't look like one.

"My ride is coming," I say. "Like any second." A flat-out lie.

"The governor might declare a state of emergency." He shakes his head. "They always talk these things up. People love drama."

People. As in, *other* people. Not him. Mac Durant doesn't

go for drama. That's the message he's trying to convey. And yet he's the one causing the drama here. I planned on hiding out for a while at the museum, but because of Mac, my safe space no longer feels safe. I should leave. Now.

I don't want to go home, but what choice do I have? I have no money, no phone. None of my friends live within walking distance. I'd probably turn to Neel at a time like this, but he and I are in a fight.

Going home doesn't mean I have to talk to my mom. I'll go straight to my room and hide under the covers. But before I can do that, I have to get Mac to leave.

I clear my throat. "I'm sure you have, you know, plans or whatever."

He doesn't answer, too busy perusing our museum wall.

I'll shut off the lights so he gets the hint. It's extreme and potentially confusing, but it's time to be bold. I override all self-loathing and slink toward the light switch. As I reach it, Mac unknowingly steps in my path and I'm forced to retreat.

"You still take the bus?" Mac says, doing a near pirouette to locate me.

"Yeah," I say, surprised that he remembers. "Unfortunately."

Mac hasn't taken the bus since middle school, and back then he was usually fast asleep on the morning ride. This is one subject I'd love to hear him elaborate on—the past, *our* past, the tiny amount we have—but he abandons the memory as abruptly as he raises it.

It's time, I decide, for the tried-and-true message sender: the yawn. As Mac browses, I make my first attempt. It's too breathy, barely audible. On my second try, I really project and wind up sounding like an elderly wizard passing a kidney stone.

"Boy," I say, dialing back the dramatics. "I'm super tired."

Mac, oblivious, checks his phone for the millionth time and returns it to his pocket. His next question is absurd, given what I've just watched him do for the past five minutes.

"Can I use your phone again?" Mac says.

Why not use yours? is a sensible response that I talk myself out of.

"Sure," I say.

He returns to the front room. I give it three Mississippis and follow, stopping at the end of the hallway, clinging to the last bit of wall. I lean slowly to the side until one of my nosy eyes gains a sliver of sight.

Mac holds the receiver low, not moving, thinking. He lifts the receiver, dials, listens. He hangs up and waits. He turns to the window. Hard to see out there.

He turns back, and I know I should be moving, but he completes his turn, and yup, half of my face is clearly visible, which is way weirder than a whole face.

"Hi," Mac says.

I step out with my whole face. "Hi."

He sits on a stool behind the counter. His elbows drop to the glass and his hands clutch the sides of his fallen head.

There's only one good reason why Mac wouldn't want to make a call from his own working phone: because he doesn't want the person he's calling to know it's him. That explains the first call to 911. But what about this new call? Who was Mac Durant calling this time?

Mac raises his head and looks at the ceiling. His torso lengthens and his neck stretches back. A deep groan putters out, and he rests his head sideways on the pillow of his unfurled palm. I watch in awe.

Dreamily, he asks: "Are your parents still together?"

The question is random and timely all at once. I shake my head. No, they're not.

"Lucky," Mac says.

Lucky? No, I don't agree. Not lucky at all. If Mac only knew what I've had to endure today precisely because my nuclear family got blown apart.

He sits tall in front of the window. Outside, the snow is dense. The flakes hold hands as they fall. You can't see through the barricade they form.

His focus shifts along the wall and holds at the front door. "They're running pretty late," Mac says.

"Who?"

"Your ride."

Oh right, my imaginary ride. "Must be the weather," I say. That seems believable.

He stands and walks out from behind the counter, his size growing as he comes, his bandaged hand dangling. I dig my back against the wall. His coat swishes loudly and then faintly as he passes by and again puts distance between us. He appears to be heading for the door. At last. Elvis is leaving the building.

But no. He walks past the door.

It's torture. I left my house feeling like the loneliest person in the world, and now I've actually got company, and it's exciting, yes, but also frightening and confusing, and the timing is all wrong.

"I need to close up," I say, nearing the end of my conversational rope. "Is there anything else I can help you with or...?"

He checks his phone—again. Is *he* the one who's waiting for someone? What the hell is going on? I can't take it anymore.

"Why are you still here?" I say.

He looks up. "Me? Why are *you* still here?"

Are you kidding? Hello! "I work here. Obviously."

"You haven't called your ride. No text. Nothing."

"That's because...I forgot my phone at home."

He smirks. "Really? There's a phone right here."

My throat squeezes. He steps closer, infringing on my space. "Not to be a dick, but I don't think anyone's coming to get you."

I touch the wall in case I need help standing. "Why would you say that?"

He points to the front door. Mac must have seen it earlier when he was by the window: the sign where the museum's hours are posted.

"You closed at four," Mac says. "It's past seven now."

In the completely bogus story I've woven, I've been off work for three hours, just waiting here patiently. Not bothering to contact anyone. Not checking for a car out the window.

Dressed like a professional couch potato. Moments ago I was in the back room cowered on the floor. Mac observed all this. And I thought *I* was an expert at paying attention.

"So?" I say.

I still don't know why any of this matters or what it is we're really talking about.

"*So*," Mac says, beginning a slow circle around the room. "Are you going to tell me why you're really here?"

My head sinks. I've been keeping it together, trying to, for months now, years really, and after the day I've had, I'm quickly coming apart.

In a quiet voice, I admit, "I don't want to go home."

He sighs. "Me neither."

I watch him. His steady circling—it now resembles nervous pacing. What should have been obvious from the start finally is: This guy, for whatever reason, can't sit still.

"Well?" Mac says, throwing his arms in the air in a kind of surrender. "Neither one of us wants to go home."

His golden eyes find mine across the room.

"Then let's not," he says.

Mac throws his coat open with the flair of a superhero and places it against the wall, on a hook that's not there. The coat falls to the floor and he seems fine with it.

"You got any snacks here?" Mac says. "A machine or whatever?"

I shake my head. He hums a song of disappointment.

I've watched Mac Durant in school, on the bus, online. There's an intensity about him always, an inexhaustible playfulness, but his energy now feels manic. He's bouncing on his heels, ready to run circles in our little hamster cage.

I recognize the shirt he's wearing. It's black with *Sneaker World* embroidered across the heart. He sees me staring at it. He reads his own chest as if he's forgotten what's written there.

"I came straight from work," he says. "I've seen you in the store before, haven't I?"

"Oh. Yeah. Probably."

I've definitely seen him. I probably passed right by Sneaker World this afternoon when Mom and I were at the mall. I just can't believe he'd remember seeing me, even vaguely. I'm pretty skilled at going unnoticed by his kind. But this is the second time he's recalled my presence somewhere.

His eyes search for something to grab on to and land back on me. "Maybe you should give me the tour."

"Yeah, sure. That'll be five dollars."

He digs through his wallet. "You got change for a twenty?"

"I was kidding." I thought that was obvious.

He pauses, shrugs, puts away his money.

It still hasn't occurred to him that I never agreed to his plan of us both staying here. "I'm sorry. I don't understand, like, what this is. The whole thing, it's just very…"

He looks at me, assuming I'm about to define *the whole thing*, but I don't. Because I can't.

"Trust me," Mac says when he accepts that I'm done speaking. "This is not how I planned on spending my night."

We can agree on that. Finally, he's acknowledging the weirdness of the situation. Also, is he insulting me? I can't tell. I can only imagine what he'd be doing tonight if he wasn't here with me. Yoga poses in a mirror. Sharing a sixer with his bros. Sexting random girls. No idea. As far as I know, he's not dating anyone. Not publicly, anyway.

"You sure there's nothing to eat here?" He leans over the counter and sniffs around like a scavenger. There may be a few souvenir mints lying around, but that's about it.

"I'll be right back," I say.

His eager face tells me he believes I'll be returning with

food. Really, I'm taking a bathroom break. I need time to process.

Alone in the bathroom, I check my eyes for tear evidence. I hope Mom is home right now worried sick about me. Pacing back and forth, biting her nails, calling everyone we know. She deserves it after what she's done.

That settles it: There's no way I'm going home so quickly. I'd rather make my mom sweat it out. I guess that means I'm staying here with Mac.

Wait. Say that again: I'm staying here with Mac Durant.

Mac Durant is the kid who got the third-most votes for class president in sixth grade and he didn't even run. In eighth grade, Brian Slatin, who was the first openly gay kid I can remember knowing, asked him to the spring dance, and Mac said yes, which pissed off girls and confused guys. Anyone who thought it was a goof for attention (as if Mac were starving for it) was proved wrong when Mac joined the LGBTQIA League freshman year.

He's straight, no doubt. He's been with some of the prettiest girls in school, including the infamous (to me) Finley Wooten. His longest relationship was with Claire Wong, who's a year ahead of us, and that lasted almost three months. She reportedly cried when he came to school last fall with a shaved head. He's probably the only person that Isla, Brooke, and I have included in one of our rounds of F, Marry, Kill who hasn't been sacrificed. No one seems willing to lose him.

He's friends with pretty much everyone. Teachers light

up when they talk to him as if they're the ones looking up to *him*. Coaches, too. Mac is supposedly so gifted an athlete that he plays for some pre-professional soccer team instead of our school team.

He zips through the halls like a gazelle, never lingering, which heightens every brief sighting of him. Passing by his house one day in the passenger seat of my mom's car, I saw him pushing a mower shirtless and have cursed myself ever since for being too slow to grab a photo. Rumor has it he does laps regularly at the YMCA, but I'm not about to wear a swimsuit in public just for a glimpse of a guy. (Okay, *maybe* Timothée Chalamet.)

There are more muscular jocks, more provocative personalities, more impressive brains, far suaver players, but none of them is the mesmerizing it-factor hybrid of wholesome and edgy, conscientious and carefree, that Mac is. It's not fair, honestly, for one person to be that blessed. People who know him best call him by his last name or sometimes Doc (a play off his initials M.D.). To me, he's only ever been Mac Durant.

Being forced to stay here with him shouldn't be seen as a punishment. It's a miracle. A life changer. How many times have I indulged in the daydream that some random hot guy would waltz into my life to save me from unending boredom? Well, it's happening. Finally. Now. He's here. For some inexplicable reason, he's here. With me. Embrace it. For once, stop overthinking and just go with it.

I smooth out my hair and ruffle it up again in a purposeful

way that seems believably accidental and head back into my fantasy/nightmare.

I find Mac in the front room, looking at one of our most popular photos. It shows the original steel tower that was built on the property, much different from the art deco replacement that stands here today.

"The Eternal Light," Mac says, reading the placard on the wall. "Is this thing for real?"

The story of the Eternal Light is not only featured prominently at the entrance of the museum but repeated verbally to every patron who tours the inside of the tower. The story goes like this: The original steel tower was built for the fiftieth anniversary celebration of Thomas Edison's light bulb in 1929. A special bulb was placed at the bottom called the Eternal Light. Edison named it that because he claimed the bulb would stay lit forever. Two years later, lightning struck the tower and it fell to the ground. Amazingly, the bulb never stopped glowing. Even more amazing, it's been lit ever since. It still glows to this day.

"Just another myth," I say, contradicting the story I've told thousands of patrons.

He looks confused.

"I mean, I wasn't there, obviously. But there's no way he made a bulb that's been lit for almost a hundred years."

He smiles. "If you hate Edison so much, why do you work here?"

This is what I get for being honest. Now I have to explain myself.

"Edison sold this image of himself as a genius, but the truth is, most of his inventions were failures and he was a terrible businessman. Like, the worst. His companies were always out of money. I just don't like when people act bigger than they are."

He nods the way you do when you don't understand and you're ready to stop trying.

But he doesn't stop. This Elvis is tireless.

"Is that how it goes?" Mac says. "When you're showing people around, are you mostly shit talking? Because I feel like I'm missing out on a killer tour."

This guy. "I'm not shit talking. I think there's some really amazing stuff in here. It's just, the story we tell, this picture we present to everyone, not all of it is . . ."

He finishes for me. "True."

We share a look. He seems to get it now. But what exactly he gets, I don't know.

"Did you just get me to crank call 911?" I say. "I'm pretty sure that's a crime."

He exhales, as if for the first time tonight. "I actually know the guy. The guy in the garage. I didn't want him to find out it was me calling. That's why I asked you to make the call. It wasn't cool of me to throw it on you like that. I'm sorry."

Oh, an apology. That's what's happening here. My body uncoils.

"It's okay," I say.

But is it? Things still don't add up. It makes sense that Mac would know the guy. He knew his address. He lives on the same street. But why would Mac care if the guy found out that he called for help? And it still doesn't explain the bruised hand. I should have demanded answers. Now it seems too late to ask.

He points to another record player. "What does this one sound like?"

The phonograph he's referring to is everyone's favorite. It's got a big ornate horn. When people imagine an old-timey music player, they're usually picturing something like this.

The tour guide in me can't help herself. I want to disprove his image of me as a bad docent. He should have seen the tips I pulled in over the summer.

"You know that phrase 'put a sock in it'?" I prepare the phonograph as I talk. "People wanted their phonographs to be louder, so the Edison company created this one. The problem was, it was *too* loud."

I start the record to show what I mean and raise my voice accordingly. I'm concerned that this sudden confidence I've found is undeserved and that I'm misreading his actual curiosity, but it's too late. I'm on autopilot, reciting a memorized script.

"Women who were hosting dinner parties didn't want their guests to have to shout to hear each other. They wanted background music. But there was no volume knob on these early machines. So how did these housewives solve the problem?"

I reach behind the player for my prop.

"They stuck a sock in it," I say, filling the sound hole with a rolled-up pair. The volume is instantly cut in half.

The typical crowd will respond here with laughs and

applause and audible *ahhs*. Mac is not my typical audience. He does none of these things.

I cut the music.

Mac stares at the phonograph long after it's been silenced. "We probably have a thousand records at my house."

The intimacy of what he's just revealed is disorienting, but there's another quality to it, something I'd describe as sadness if I thought Mac Durant was susceptible to such a thing.

He turns to me. "You have a nice voice."

Every time he speaks, the universe reshapes itself. What new world am I in now?

"Say something," Mac commands.

Suddenly, I can't think of a single good word to say. "Cool...pizza...baby..."

Mac laughs. "It's like that actress. The blond."

That narrows it down.

"She's in those superhero movies," Mac says. "But her hair is, like, pink or something."

I have the answer, but it can't possibly be the right one. "Scarlett Johansson?"

"Yes! Her!"

It's as if I just identified an obscure celebrity from the twenties (which I can actually do—museum girl) and not one of the biggest current stars on the planet. ScarJo plays Black Widow, whose hair is technically red (most of the time; Neel can explain why the color changes across the Avengers series). But we're not talking about hair here.

"I really like it," Mac says about my voice.

I suddenly want to assault him with syllables, but I'm too shocked to move my lips. I'm not used to compliments from guys who aren't Neel. Also, I've never liked the sound of my own voice, deeper than most girls'. I always sound bored and lethargic, like a person waking from a ten-year coma and realizing that they're not all that excited to be alive again.

"I don't think I've heard you say more than two words the whole time I've known you," Mac says.

Has he ever known me?

"Thank you," I say, feeling super uncomfortable. "I'm quiet, I guess."

But there's more to it, and Mac senses that, his mind chewing on something.

I change the subject. "I guess I could give you the official tour if you really want," I hear myself say, testing out my *nice* voice.

"Okay," Mac says, nodding as if he doesn't care one way or another. "But listen..."

I am listening. I really am.

"I'm starving. I didn't get a chance to eat dinner."

Tell me about it. Skipping dinner is why I'm here.

"Let's grab something," Mac says.

"You mean, out there?"

The windows are whited out. It's like peering through the glass of a running washing machine.

"We should go now," Mac says, reaching for his coat. "Before the weather gets even worse."

Well. Okay, then.

3:23 PM

Charlie was clacking on his silent keyboard in the living room, the sound streaming only to his headphones. Sheet music rested on the stand in front of him, songs to be played at tonight's wedding. His back was to me, but I would have bet anything he wasn't looking at the sheets. He usually played with eyes closed and a goofy smile, head bopping for an imaginary crowd of hundreds.

I lay on the couch behind him with my phone. Before Charlie moved in, the living room was neutral territory. Now with his keyboard here, even pressed against the wall and silenced (mostly), it felt like I was invading *his* space. I could have gone up to my bedroom, but sometimes I just need a change of scenery.

I scanned social media while I waited for Neel to text me. It had been only a few hours since we'd seen each other at the mall, but our conversation had been one of those messy types that can only be erased by having a new, clean one.

The front door burst open, sending a rush of frigid air

into the house. Charlie glanced over his shoulder. Mom dropped two grocery bags inside, disappeared, and returned with two more bags before sealing the door shut.

"It was a madhouse," Mom said, hooting like a fatigued owl. "There were whole shelves that were totally empty."

"What's for dinner?" I said.

"Well," she said, ramping up the word for optimum anticipation. "I'm making a special meal."

I lowered my phone. "What do you mean *you're* making it?"

"I'm making it."

"Why isn't Charlie making it?"

On cue, Charlie's tapping grew more insistent, as if he was taking a solo at the concert in his mind.

"Come talk to me in the kitchen," Mom said. She carried the groceries away, forcing me to unglue myself from my resting place. "Grab those bags, please," she called out.

As I reached for the bags, I stepped directly into one of her snowy footprints, and my sock got wet. Now I was extra annoyed.

"Charlie has a gig, so I'm cooking," Mom said once I arrived in the kitchen. "I told you this morning we were doing something special."

"Why aren't we getting takeout?"

"What for?"

"Because that's what we always do."

"I can't cook a meal?" Mom said, laughing it off.

"You *can*. You just don't."

"Well, tonight I am. I'm cooking."

Something was going on here and I decided I didn't like it. I dropped the bags on the floor harder than I meant to.

"Sweetie, what's better than chicken soup on a day like this?"

There it was, her big surprise. She waited wide-eyed and smiling. I could have answered her ridiculous question if she really wanted me to, but I didn't have the energy. I headed for the stairs.

In my bedroom, I changed my wet sock but left the dry one on. It didn't matter that the two didn't match. I wasn't seeing anyone tonight, except maybe a food delivery person if I was lucky.

I exchanged messages with Isla and Brooke on our group text, each of us wondering why it never seemed to snow this much on school days. Brooke was riding out the storm at her dad's (it being his weekend), and she was texting me on the side about her DM relationship with Anton Metza, which for some reason she hadn't yet told Isla about. I'd known my girlfriends much longer than I'd known Neel, but in many ways my friendship with him was easier. It was more honest and *usually* less dramatic.

Earlier at the mall, Neel had exploded on me out of nowhere, saying I was acting crazy. How come when a girl speaks her mind in a passionate way, she's acting crazy? I expected that type of bullshit from everyone else, but not my best friend.

I broke the silence now with a text: *Still out with Ezra?*

Ezra is Neel's *other* friend. His little smoke buddy.

Neel replied: *Still in with Nightshade?*

Saying that to me in a text, it wasn't okay.

Neel could be, for better or worse, excitable. Better when you presented him with a brilliant idea for the inventors fair. Worse when, well, right about now.

We met in eighth grade in a group called New Beginnings, and ever since, I've looked to him as my personal guru in all aspects of life. Not guru as in a master (and not because he's Indian)—more like a highly overqualified assistant. In our relationship, I'm the boss. I value and appreciate his input, but ultimately I call the shots.

I thought of all the things I could write back to him, but it wouldn't make a difference. Instead, I opened my computer and read some new messages that had come in. Time slipped away.

Before leaving for his gig, Charlie poked his head into my room and urged me in his subtle way to go back downstairs to talk to Mom. I did, and it was a mistake. If I knew what she had in store for me, I never would have left my bedroom.

You weren't always quiet. Much younger, you would go up to kids on the playground and introduce yourself. You put yourself out there. No shame.

Mom swears you were confident, strong-willed, unafraid to voice your opinion. At a parent conference in kindergarten, the teacher reported that you were sometimes too chatty, especially when paired with Isla. The two of you had to be separated.

Then, a quieting. It happens around eight, nine. Suddenly the one tiny difference between you and them is all they can focus on. But your hand is only part of the story. It's nothing compared with your broken heart. Once your dad is gone, forget it, you practically go mute. You're thirteen, so it could be perceived as typical teen girl bullshit. When you do speak, your tone is biting. An edge to every remark. Or it's a joke. Mostly you're silent. Silent for days. Mom sees your wheels turning.

Talk to me, she says.

You don't know how.

Talk to me.

Where do you start?

Talk to me.

Your mouth won't open.

It's easier to speak up on social media, but even there it takes time to find your voice. You try out several profiles to see which one fits best.

Totes Tegan: Your fun-loving, super-optimistic alter ego. Wowed by everything from video games to worms on a sidewalk. Inspirational one-liners like "Do something today that your future self will thank you for."

Weekend Tour Guide: Life at work. Fun trivia about Thomas Edison. Stuff to make your dad proud. Also with an aim to get people to come to the museum. Maybe if they see you in action, they'll look at you differently. No students come. Your friends don't count.

Sriracha Girl: You leave your name off this account. The motif is food covered in sriracha. Pretzels and sriracha.

Grapes and sriracha. Coffee and sriracha. For effect, not consumption. But no one feels the effect. What was your point again with this one?

We're All Gonna Die: Melting glaciers! Destroyed habitats! Endangered species! It's doomsday every day. Again, no mention of Tegan Everly on the account. Not even your close friends know this account is yours. Your photo of the last living white rhino gets nineteen likes, which is practically going viral for you. Meanwhile Mom gets likes in the midhundreds for her posts showing how it's possible to find love again. Good for her.

Neel thinks you're going about social media all wrong. *What makes you truly unique?*

You struggle to answer him.

Your hand, he says. *Put it out there. Flaunt it.*

You hate him for this.

The fact is, you're already sort of popular. Just for the dumbest reason. Tegan Everly is the girl with the hand. Everyone knows that. But who wants to be reduced to something so inconsequential? It's a small part of what makes you you. Why make it the main focus? There are people in the world who choose to put their limb difference on display: YouTubers, podcasters, authors, athletes. As much as you sort of admire these figures, you've never understood how they do it or why they'd even want to.

Neel means well. But no, you're not going to "flaunt it." You're not engaging in inspiration porn.

When your best friend can't understand, no one can. You try to talk to Neel, to Isla and Brooke, to your mom, to the professionals you're sent to, but you don't know how to say what you really feel. The only one you can talk to is your dad. You can email him and say exactly how you feel about everything, no matter what it is, and he'll never tell you you're wrong. He just listens, and when he writes you back, he tells you only what you need to hear.

Dad,

I got a job for the summer at the Edison Center. I'm
pretty sure Maggie only hired me because of you. You
practically kept the place in business, so I guess she
owes you. I'm way underqualified, but I'm learning.
Paying attention like you taught me. The place is
pretty much the same as you'd remember it—boring.
Just kidding.

Love,
Tegan

Tegan,

That's my girl! I used to love to drag you there. Our
little Smithsonian. Can you believe one man could
accomplish so much? It breaks my heart that more
people don't take the time to visit. It's right there
under their noses!

Stop being so hard on yourself. I bet you're great.

Love,
Dad

Dad,

There's something about being at the museum. I
guess it reminds me of you. All the times you brought
me along. It's nice to have a place like that. Especially
when the house feels a little crowded. Sometimes I
just need to get out.

Love,
Tegan

Tegan,

Trust me. I understand. Remember when I'd go for
those long walks and Mom would get mad because
she needed me for something and I never had my
phone with me? Maybe you didn't realize it at the
time, but that was just me needing space. We all
need that. You find it wherever you can.

Love,
Dad

I t's already deep, several inches. You would think it hadn't snowed in years and the backed-up supply was all being sent down now. The cold is brisk and the wind fierce, but I can barely feel the elements. I'm doing what I set out to do: I'm going with it. Seeing where the night takes me.

It's taking me on a spontaneous walk with the one and only Mac Durant. Isla and Brooke will never believe it. I can hardly believe it myself. Sure, I've been critical about Mac and his kind in the past, with good reason. But I don't want to think about that right now. I just want to be in the moment.

When we leave the museum, Mac points to the memorial tower on the terrace. Its height, more than 130 feet, is impressive, but what seems to draw his eye through the snow is the beaming brightness at its apex.

"The world's largest light bulb," I tell him. "Right here in New Jersey. Nearly twice the height of the tallest basketball player. Inside the tower, at the way bottom, is the Eternal Light."

Mac makes no comment as we pass by. Maybe now that we're out of the museum, the historical trivia isn't going to cut it. I decide not to say another word until he does.

Minutes later, we're on Route 27 and I'm practically sweating. He's the fastest walker I've ever seen and completely unaware of how much I'm struggling to keep up with him. Still, it feels good to get moving. Dad was right about walking: It clears your head.

There's no pedestrian path here, so we hug the side of the salted street. The occasional car maneuvers around us. Headlights briefly reveal two nutjobs on the road. One without a jacket.

That would be Mac. He's braving the cold in just his long-sleeve work shirt. When he found out I didn't have a coat, he insisted I wear his. Full disclosure: It may be the thrill of wearing Mac's garment, more than the fabric itself or our furious pace, that's keeping me warm.

I feel around inside his pockets. He removed his phone, but there are other treasures. A stiff paper rectangle, perhaps a loyalty card for his favorite burger spot. Some type of hard candy, or just really old gum. A set of keys. And finally, no pocket is complete without a few pieces of miscellaneous lint.

I play with Mac's lint as I walk beside him. His body may not feel the cold, but his mind is fully aware of it.

"Snow White. Jon Snow. That President Snow dude from *Hunger Games*."

He rattles off these names without warning. Having finished his list, he turns to me.

"Edward Snowden?" I guess, only mildly confident that I understand the rules of his game.

"Good one," Mac says.

I'm a natural, apparently. I quickly arrive at a second name, Simon Snow from the novel *Fangirl* and others, a character I'm fairly confident Mac has never heard of, but he cuts me off with a new question.

"You think it's true about snowflakes? That no two are the same?"

"I guess," I say. He's hard to keep up with in more ways than one. Since the moment he stepped into the museum, I've had trouble catching up to him. Swallowing my pride, I ask, "Can we slow down?"

He looks over and sees that I'm out of breath. "Sorry," he says in a way that suggests this isn't the first time he's been asked to apply the brakes.

He adjusts his stride, but his mouth speeds along. "All I'm saying is, they'd have to study every single snowflake to know for sure. You think out of the millions of snowflakes that are falling right now, just in this one town, there's not a chance two of them are a match?"

He gazes up at the busy sky, faithful in his belief. This conversation reminds me of the type I normally have with Neel, which is shocking. On the spectrum of possible personalities, Mac and Neel have to be at opposite ends. Like, even if they both somehow worked for SpaceX, Neel would be crunching numbers back at home base while Mac piloted the rocket past the stars.

I give Mac the answer Neel might give *me* if I asked him the same question. "There are too many possible variables. It's like when people talk about the universe being infinite and what if there's another Earth exactly like ours somewhere. Let's say there is, and on the other Earth you and I are doing the same thing we're doing right now, walking to a store in the snow. Even on that planet, where everything is ninety-nine point nine nine percent alike, do you think the other me and the other you would be having this exact same conversation?"

"Why not?" Mac says.

He has this way of sounding clueless and enlightened all at once, and I can't begin to understand how he does it.

"Because we could be talking about anything," I say. "We could be talking about rock climbing or pistachios or vaudeville."

"We could be talking about mailboxes."

"Um, yeah, sure."

"Or why you would leave the house in a snowstorm without a jacket."

I turn to him.

"I mean, I know you're a bit of a hard-ass," Mac says, "but still."

I stop in the road and let go of his lint. "What the hell does *that* mean? How am I a hard-ass?"

He hesitates, his smile cowering. "Well, *kind* of how you're acting right now?"

I roll my eyes and walk away.

Mac jogs to catch up. A set of tires sizzles the wet road as a lonely car zips by. Once it's safe, we cross the street to the sidewalk. Here the snow is untouched. The only sound is our shoes flattening snow and my (Mac's) coat swishing. My mind turns. Deep inside I knew that going along with Mac tonight was a risk. The danger was part of the appeal. Still, I feel like I was just sucker punched.

I have to ask, "Is that what people say about me?"

"No," Mac insists, trying to play it off. "It's just a vibe I get, that's all."

He's not squirming out of this. I need more. "What vibe?"

When he finally speaks, it's with delicacy. "Just that you can't be bothered. You know, with people."

I've been described in a similar way before: tough, guarded, standoffish. By parents and friends. An occupational therapist once called me "headstrong" and swore it was a compliment, but it didn't feel like one. It's not that I *want* to be distant from people. I'm just careful about who I'm willing to let myself get close to, who's really worth it. And honestly, Mac has it backward; a lot of the time it seems people can't be bothered with *me*.

Meanwhile, look at Mac. He's so eager to take on the world, he can't slow down. There's nothing up ahead that could possibly harm him. It's fascinating to witness, even inspiring. But it also makes me think that he and I exist on totally different planet Earths and that the galaxy between us is too vast to meet anywhere in the middle.

"I'm serious," Mac says, maintaining an apologetic air. "I haven't heard anyone talk shit about you. There's no Nightshade rumor going around or anything like that."

I really want to see his face when he says this, but I force myself to keep looking forward. If there was a Nightshade rumor about me, I'd definitely know about it. "It's fine," I say. "Let's just keep going."

It's a whole bunch of awkward silence until we spot distant neon lights. Our closest option for commerce is EZ Mart, and that's where we land.

Inside the store, a lift in temperature brings relief. Mac shakes the snow dandruff off his head. I'm not ready to remove my hood just yet. With warmth comes the realization that I have to pee—badly. I dart off to the bathroom only to find the handle locked and a sign on the door.

Mac notices my agitation when I return. "What's wrong?"

"Bathroom is out of order. I really have to go." I'm mad at myself for not doing it back at the museum—when I was *literally* standing in the bathroom.

We scope out the aisles. It's the most random collection of items. Plungers. Dog collars. Pregnancy tests. Bike locks.

For food, I go with comfort: pretzels, licorice, Oreos. Also, sriracha-flavored Doritos. I'm hungrier than I knew. Mac selects two energy bars, beef jerky, and a too-green banana.

Most of the water is gone from the refrigerated section. Bought up by storm preppers. It's eerie. A bottled Frappuccino calls out to me, and I answer it.

I meet Mac at the register with my hands full. Fresh humiliation arrives. "I just realized I don't have money."

"You should have let me pay you for the tour," Mac teases. "No worries. It's on me."

His stuff is lined up on the counter, but he's not ready to check out yet. "I want to look for one more thing," he says, and leaves.

I place my snacks on the counter next to his. I count up my items to make sure I haven't grabbed more things than he has. The clerk watches me in my hood, unsure whether to wait or start ringing us up. There doesn't seem to be any rush. We're the only ones here.

I turn away from the register. A pair of headlights beams into the store as a car pulls into the lot. When the headlights shut off, I get a clear view out the window. It's the same car that was parked in my driveway earlier today.

I drop to the floor like a military recruit, unnerving the watchful clerk. I forget for a moment that I'm already hidden inside Mac's oversized parka. I scamper away and wait, crouched low behind a rack of gummy bears and chocolate-covered nuts until I hear the door jingle open. When I see the big shiny collar of Charlie's shirt pass by, I shoot out the door before it has a chance to close behind him.

Outside, I take one more look inside EZ Mart, and I run.

I 'm tucked behind bushes on the side of the road when I see someone with two plastic bags race by.

"Mac!" I shout.

He returns and his eyes widen. "What are you doing?"

Good question. I started running (or sliding, more accurately) in the direction of the museum, but then, realizing I never said goodbye and how rude and shady that might seem, I decided to dive into this row of shrubbery. Which I'm now unable to remove myself from.

"Help me up," I say.

He reaches out his hand, but it's aimed at my left side, so I have to roll over like a bowling ball before I can take hold of him with my other hand. A portion of me, even in this frenzied moment, shudders from his touch, the thrill of the two of us touching, but mostly I feel like puffed-up deadweight in need of assistance.

I get upright, finally, and insist we save the talking for later.

We pass a row of corporate buildings and turn into the

train station. A frigid metal bench is where we find rest. The awning above grants us temporary peace from the weather.

Once we're seated, Mac addresses the obvious with gentle gravity. "Is there someone looking for you?"

The embarrassment I feel about running off like that is tempered by the surprising concern I hear in his voice. I catch my breath. "Maybe."

We're both winded, but Mac's weariness doesn't appear related to the demands of the run we just took. "I didn't know where you went, so I asked the clerk if he saw the girl I was with. This guy behind me, I didn't see him there, he says, 'What girl?'"

"And what did you say?"

"I lied. I don't know why. The guy was just really big and..."

"Black?"

"No. Well, yeah, but that's not—"

"Sure," I say, reveling just a smidge in seeing Mr. No-Big-Deal look so flustered. "Anyway, keep going. What did you tell him?"

"I made up a name. Samantha. That's my cousin's name."

"Then what?"

"I paid and left, and now I'm here with you," Mac says, ending his tale.

Charlie is supposed to be in Princeton tonight. That's a forty-five-minute drive from here with clear skies. He left for his gig over four hours ago. I watched him go. I said goodbye. He wouldn't ditch his band in the middle of a wedding. They're like family to him. Mom must have caught him before he hit the stage and told him what happened. He probably had no choice but to race home. She must have sounded that distraught. I hate the thought of poor Charlie being out in this storm because of me, but I can't deny the satisfaction I feel making my mom pay for what she did.

"Listen," Mac says, demonstrating a sensitivity I'm amazed to learn comes so naturally to him. "I'm not trying to get in your business or whatever."

"But..."

"But if you're in some kind of situation..."

"You mean like a big black guy chasing me?"

"Not funny."

No, it isn't. And for reasons Mac isn't aware of. But I couldn't resist teasing him. It *is* kind of funny (and fun) for Mac to finally be the one forced to catch up with me. To watch him have to choose his words carefully, which is my minute-by-minute reality. He's finally out of his comfort zone.

Anyway, I can't be too hard on him. For some unknown reason, he's still here.

"Thanks," I say.

"For what?" Mac wonders.

"For covering for me. And coming after me."

I started off the night feeling so alone, and now the feeling isn't nearly as bad.

"We made a plan," Mac says, as if it means something to

him, and this makes it okay to let it mean something to me, too. "Besides, I can't eat all these snacks by myself."

I look at the bags at his feet. "Really? I feel like you could."

"Yeah, I totally could." I see his smile underneath, and it settles me.

A train roars its horn as it nears our tiny commuter station. How much snow does it take to stop the trains from running? How much snow forces a wedding to be canceled?

The train slows, its wheels screeching. A flood of people exit while only one woman waits to board. I imagine that the woman is me when I'm older. I'm making my way home. Do I live in a house? An apartment? What type of job do I have? What kind of life? It's hard to see my future with any clarity.

"If you didn't live here in Edison, where would you want to live?" I say. "Do you ever think about that?"

"England or Spain." It's a lightning-quick answer and he knows it. "That's where the best football clubs in the world are. *Soccer*, sorry. I sound like a douche."

No, he doesn't. Not really. "That's your thing, right? Soccer?"

"Sometimes it's all I think about." He seems tortured by this.

"They say you're good."

"Who says?"

"Everybody."

He doubts it.

"Why is that surprising?" I say.

"I know for a fact it's not 'everybody' saying that." I wait for him to explain what he means, but he only adds, "Everything's up in the air right now. For the first time in forever I don't have a team to play for."

His expression is blank, but I hear the discomfort in his voice. Beyond the awning hangs a falling curtain of twinless snowflakes.

"Why don't you play for our school?" I say.

"It's sort of a waste of time. Anyone who's serious plays club soccer."

Okay, now maybe he sounds a little arrogant. This is the Mac I know from afar. The kind of person who has no doubts about his own value. That must be nice.

But just as I think I have him pegged, he squirms out of the box I put him in.

"Europe is just a fantasy," Mac says. "I'd be lucky to ride the bench for a division two school. I just want a scholarship somewhere. I'll probably end up at Rutgers, which is fine, I guess, but…"

"But what?"

"I doubt I'd make their team as a walk-on, and also, it's a little close."

Just twenty minutes away from Edison by car. Still, the way my grades have been slipping the last few years, I'd be lucky to go to Rutgers. At one point it was a certainty that I'd attend, back when my dad was teaching there and my tuition would have been waived.

I'm eager to start fresh somewhere new, but I'm not sure why Mac would be so quick to leave what he has here. I mean, Edison is boring and all, and being white in an American town that Neel says is a prized destination to Indians halfway across the world is challenging. (I know, I know, poor white people.) But Mac is like the king of this town. Or one of the kings.

"What college would you want to go to if you had your pick?" I ask.

"I don't know. Maybe Penn State. My brother's there now."

James Durant. He was a senior last year, and from what I observed, he's nothing like Mac. Super serious, never smiles. Not as attractive, either. Hence the attitude, maybe?

"I'd have to get my grades up first," Mac says, without that outsized optimism I'm used to seeing. His lack of spirit somehow feels like my fault.

"Edison didn't go to college," I say. "He didn't even go to high school. It worked out for him. My dad told me that fact. And then he regretted telling me. College professor, so, yeah, what do you expect?"

Mac doesn't respond. The longer he's silent, the more self-conscious I become.

I look across the tracks, mostly because I can't see left or right in this hood without rotating my entire existence sideways. Now that the fear and adrenaline have calmed in my body, I'm realizing I still have to pee.

"We should keep moving," Mac says.

I heave myself over and notice that he's shivering.

"You can have your coat back," I say.

He reaches into a shopping bag and removes a clear plastic

pouch. He opens it and snaps the plastic at the air. It's a poncho. He slides it over his clothes and pulls on the hood.

"I'm good," he says.

He looks ridiculous and I like it.

Waterproof now, he asks me, "You mind if we take the long way back?"

The long way back takes us up Morton Road. I'm only realizing now, as I'm struggling to climb this snowy slope with flat-bottomed sneakers, how steep this street is.

Several times Mac offers his hand to help me, but he's on my shy side. It's unfortunate how my hand has to appear in and out of my consciousness like a confused chameleon, blending into the background when I'm among friends and jumping into the foreground when meeting strangers. If I was with Neel right now, for example, it would be the last thing on my mind. But I'm with Mac.

At the top of the hill, he stops and points across the street. "You ever go sledding over there?"

It's impossible to see where he's pointing, hard as I try to make it out in the misty atmosphere. "No. Where?"

"Behind that house there's a crazy drop. My brother and I used to go when we were kids. Usually it was him and his friends. I'd tag along."

Even though he's describing boys at play, the boyish

playfulness he's sported for most of the night is missing. In its place, a weight. I never got the impression when James was in our school last year that he and Mac were tight. Most people wouldn't guess they were brothers.

"Are you guys close?" I say.

Mac turns away from the house. "Not super, no. But we're cool."

He nods, confirming it for himself, and walks off. Very quickly he remembers to wait up for me. He offers an apology smile while I catch up.

"I did go tubing once," I say.

"Once?" Mac says.

"At *least* once."

"Not into winter sports, then."

I kick up snow. "Oh no. I am extremely dispassionate about all sports."

He shakes his head in exaggerated horror.

"No offense," I add.

"I'm not offended. You just don't get it."

"Excuse me?"

"Have you ever been to a professional game of any kind?"

The answer is no.

"I guarantee if you sat in the stands and watched, you'd know what I'm talking about. I'm not saying you'd start loving soccer or whatever. But you'd see how other people can love it. Because you're watching these people who are so dedicated, who really care about what they do, and that kind of passion, it's just...powerful."

He checks to see if I understand. I do. He couldn't have explained it better.

It occurs to me only now that maybe not every guy who plays sports is a jock. Mac not playing for the school team means he can't benefit from one of the main perks of jockdom—visibility. He clearly loves watching sports, but I'm not sure how much he cares about being watched while playing them. He's some kind of sports purist.

We turn down a street that leads back to our neighborhood. I still can't believe I'm walking next to Mac Durant on a Saturday night, just the two of us. I'm not sure why he'd purposely add time to our return journey when he's lacking warm layers, but I choose not to question it. This night has already gone in so many unexpected directions that I feel woozy. But also, I've never felt more alert. I have plans tonight. Plans with Mac.

Staring ahead, Mac asks, "Are you going to tell me who that guy was?"

A street sign reads WATCH CHILDREN, and suddenly I'm worried that we're the children being watched.

"Charlie Most," I say.

"Am I supposed to know who that is?"

"You might if you were into crashing weddings."

He drops the grocery bags in the snow and blows warm air onto his hands. The bandage I applied serves as a makeshift glove.

"I can hold the bags if you want," I say, realizing I might not be pulling my weight on this adventure of ours. To be fair, this trip wasn't my idea in the first place.

He takes out his phone and stares at the bright screen. I watch a decision being made—whether to check for a message that's come in or compose a message to send out. But to whom? A girl? A guy? A mother? A father? So many possibilities. A moment ago the universe was just Mac and I and a whole lot of snow. His phone is a cruel reminder that there's a world out there full of other people.

Mac tucks his phone back into his pocket, never actually engaging with it. "I got it," he says under his breath.

He means the bags. He picks them up and moves on.

But it's hard for me to keep moving when I realize we're turning onto Anchorage Road. It's the street Mac lives on. The same street where Mac saw the guy in the garage.

"Where are we going?"

"I have to make a quick stop," Mac says.

"But where?"

"Here."

We've paused in front of a tan house partly hidden behind a mighty tree. I've traveled past this house a hundred times, always wondering what goes on inside, curious which window belongs to Mac.

I throw off my hood, suddenly sweaty. There's no number on Mac's house, but the one to the right is 90 and the one to the left is 86, and that makes this one 88. It's the address I gave the dispatcher on the 911 call.

"Why are we here?" I say.

"I live here."

"But you said you..."

"What? What's wrong?"

"You didn't want to go home. You said that."

"Yeah, well, old habits die hard," Mac says helplessly.

He starts up the driveway.

"Wait. Where are you going?"

"Inside," Mac says. "Come on."

I grab his poncho. I had a feeling when Mac had me call 911, but I pushed the feeling away, buried it deep down. I couldn't let myself consider what the call might be about—*who* the call was about.

"Who was the guy in the garage?" I say. "The guy you said you saw. The one who was trying to hurt himself."

Mac dips his head. "I'll tell you later."

"No, I need to know."

"When we get back," Mac says, pulling away. "We'll be in and out."

"Please. You have to tell me."

"I said I would. What's your problem?"

He doesn't understand. It can't wait any longer. I need to know the truth. Because what Mac doesn't know is that the truth might have something to do with me.

"You made me get on the phone," I say. "I did that for you. Just tell me who he is. That's all I'm asking. The guy in the garage, was it—"

"My dad."

Inside me an alarm sounds. The volume is deafening. I want to bend over in pain, but I can't, I know I can't, I have to remain absolutely still, I must, so as not to give myself away.

"Oh," I say.

Already a night of surprises, and here now is the worst of them. It's the beginning of my nightmare—and the end of the lie I've been living.

It's true that you're quiet. At school, especially. At school, quiet is the Tegan most people know.

But there's another Tegan. Another you. A you with a loud, powerful voice. Everyone in school knows this loud, powerful voice. But they don't know it belongs to you. No one has figured out who it is. The voice has no face. Only a name: Nightshade.

Some call Nightshade a hero. But others don't see it that way. To them, Nightshade is a troll. A bully. A villain.

Mac is one of these other people. You know this without having to ask. You know this because weeks before this night, he became one of your unlucky targets.

I s your dad...okay?" I ask, my feet firmly planted on Mac's unshoveled driveway.

Mac winces like he's got a migraine and I blasted a spotlight in his eyes. "I'm sure he is," he mutters, dissatisfied with the answer, or merely annoyed to have to report it.

"How do you know?"

"I called home before at the museum."

"But I didn't hear you talk to anybody."

"My dad answered, and I hung up."

People have been whispering for years that Mac's dad has a drinking problem. These were merely rumors—until a video went around.

"Did the ambulance ever come?" I say.

"I have no idea," Mac says, looking more and more exhausted. "I was with you. I texted him before, but he hasn't responded."

"What about your mom?"

"She's sleeping at my aunt's house tonight."

Now he's got all the answers. I don't know why I didn't

ask sooner. (Actually, I do know—I was afraid of what he might say.)

"Listen," Mac says. "I'm freezing, and I really don't want to stay here any longer than I have to. Please, let's go inside. It'll only take a second. I promise I'll explain everything to you after."

This plan might sound reasonable to the innocent outsider, but I'm an insider and far from innocent. "I'll wait out here."

"You're acting crazy right now. Just come in already."

Another guy calling me crazy. I shake my head. I'm staying put.

He looks up at the house. "My dad's probably passed out. He won't even know we're here."

Is that supposed to make me feel better about going inside?

"Besides," he says, turning back, "I thought you had to pee."

"I'm good," I say. I'd rather wet myself.

"Whatever," Mac says. "I'll leave the door open in case you change your mind. Bathroom is inside on the right." He pauses for a deep breath. "Be right back."

His poncho flares out like a see-through cape as he strides up the driveway and onto his porch. He swings open the screen door but delays at the main door. He digs through each of his pants pockets. His keys! I retrieve them from his coat pocket and walk up to the porch.

"Here," I whisper.

He reacts with relief and unlocks the door. Before going

inside, he gives me one more chance to change my mind. I shake my head. He rolls his eyes and vanishes.

I'd love to see what Mac Durant's house is like on the inside, but engaging with people's messy lives online is one thing and facing it in the flesh is another. It's too much, too real, too fast.

I wait on the porch, hugging myself for warmth. Mac could totally change his mind when he's in there and decide to stay home instead, leaving me out here shivering by my lonesome like a fool.

Headlights appear as a car creeps down Anchorage. I wonder whether the careful speed is due to the slick roads or because the driver's on the lookout for someone.

The car glides nearer. My hand takes hold of the cold latch on the screen door. Behind it, the front door is wide open. I try to make out what kind of car it is, but I can't see past the bright lights. When the car that might be Charlie's is almost upon me, I enter Mac's house.

There's light ahead, but the hallway is dark. I turn right and find the bathroom. I go in and lock the door behind me. I don't bother turning on the light. First, I pee. It's painful before it's satisfying. Once I'm empty, I remain seated, pants at my ankles, in complete darkness.

I listen. The house is silent. I'm scared that if I flush, someone will hear it. Then again, I can't leave my pee in Mac Durant's toilet. That's not a thing I can do.

I wipe and pull up my pants. I unlock the door and open it just an inch. Directly across is a set of stairs. Farther away is an unlit living room. Above me, footsteps. Before I can strategize, the footsteps barrel down the stairs. I pull the bathroom door shut so Mac won't see me.

It doesn't work as planned.

"Tegan," he says through the door.

"Just a minute," I say.

I flush, wash my hands, and meet him in the hallway. His clear poncho is gone, replaced with a proper winter jacket. His backup coat. An army-green wool hat lies haphazardly on his head.

His smile is cocky. He knew I'd eventually cave and come inside. I'm a little embarrassed to have lost that battle. Mac turns every trivial exchange into a meaningful competition.

He heads toward the kitchen. I take a moment and peer up the dark stairs. All is quiet. I guess Mac was right. His dad must be asleep.

Gazing into the void, I almost lose track of Mac. He opens a door and disappears. I hurry to catch up, not wanting to be left alone in this unfamiliar place. At the door I find stairs leading down to a dimly lit basement. I listen once more for a sound from above. Nothing. I follow Mac down.

When I reach the bottom, there's no sight of Mac. The basement is unfinished. A lone light bulb on an exposed wooden beam casts shadows over naked cement walls. There's a washer and dryer and shelves full of sporting equipment. Hockey sticks and collapsed nets. Balls of all sizes and colors, some in need of air.

Mac slips out from behind a hanging bedsheet that serves as an improvised partition. He walks past me to a tall armoire, removes a folded blanket, and steps back around the sheet. I catch a glimpse of an entertainment console with a record player and bookshelves containing rows and rows of vinyl. Mac wasn't kidding when he said his family owned a lot of records.

I step closer for a better view. A patterned rug. A crowded coffee table. It's like a little apartment. Mac's back is turned to me, the blanket hanging from his outstretched arms. He drapes it gently over a couch. Poking out from beneath the blanket is a man's head, eyes closed.

I head for the stairs. Climbing out of the basement, I turn and find Mac right behind me. We surface together in the kitchen. He pays me no mind, still focused on completing whatever mission he's on. As far as he knows, I saw nothing in the basement. A whole lot of nothing.

I see something now in the light of the kitchen. Mac is holding a large glass bottle with a clear liquid inside. Alcohol of some kind.

With his free hand, he digs through an open fridge and finds a lone chicken finger that he savagely tears in half with his teeth. He offers me the cold remainder. I shake my head no thanks.

"You sure?" Mac says. "From Flannigan's. Super good."

How can he eat at a time like this? Isn't this, like, the scene of a crime or something? For all we know, paramedics were standing in this very room a few short hours ago, wondering about the anonymous caller who tipped them off to the situation.

"Shouldn't we be going?" I say at a volume so low I'm surprised Mac can hear me.

His mouth is too busy devouring the chicken finger. Or maybe he's buying time to figure out how to break the news to me: Our plans have been canceled. I'm on my own again.

"It's fine if you feel like staying," I say. "I totally get it. It's cool. I'll let myself out."

"Damn," Mac says, trying to finish chewing. "Give me a sec. I'm coming."

I've annoyed him, I see, but it's all good—a small price to pay for not being abandoned.

He shuts the fridge and looks around the kitchen one last time. I get a head start for the exit.

At the front door, I loop the handles of our EZ Mart bags around my wrists, plunk my hands into my coat pockets—Mac's pockets—and elbow open the screen door. I take one last look inside Mac's house, all but certain I'll never be back.

Mac locks up. The alcohol bottle sticks brazenly out of his jacket pocket.

We walk in silence to the end of the driveway. Reaching the curb, he bends down and starts digging through a random snow pile. When the cold gets too extreme, he pauses to blow on his hands, and then digs some more.

"What are you doing?" I say.

He holds something out to me. I take the snow-covered object and realize from its gritty texture and blunt weight that it's a brick. There are more bricks. A whole pile. Mac grabs one for himself.

"Should we toss it through the window?" he says.

I don't get the joke.

"Nothing will happen. I promise."

73

He's smiling, but there's no glow of humor on his face, only a vacant stare.

"We should go," I say.

My request doesn't reach him.

"Mac."

He snaps his head my way—sudden recognition. He lets the brick fall, as if quitting a long fight.

I leave my brick with his. "What is this?" I say, gesturing to the pile.

"My mailbox," Mac says. "It was until a few hours ago. Before my dad ran it over with his car."

I stand at the end of Mac's driveway and picture how it might have happened. His dad behind the wheel, whatever shape he was in. The car leveling the hardy structure. The wreckage visible on the grass until the snow came to cover it. Was his dad hurt? Was Mac in the car? What the hell is going on? Suddenly, the two of us walking out of here together like it's no big deal seems unlikely.

"Do you need to stay here? With your dad?"

"No. Definitely not." Mac steps away from the curb, as if I might try to force him to remain here. "If you feel like going home, that's fine, but—"

"I'm not saying that."

He repositions his hat on his head. "Cool. Let's head back to the museum."

Is there nowhere else we can go? As much as I'd like to spend more time with Mac, being at the Edison Center adds this weird pressure: like I'm the host and it's my responsibility to entertain.

"There's not much to do there," I say. "It's really small and—"

"We still haven't had dinner," Mac says, his smile returning, bright and true. Once again, he seems more than willing to lead the way.

I look at the bags around my wrists. He takes one of them so we're sharing the load.

"Plus, we have a lot to talk about," Mac says.

"We do?"

"I want to hear more about the famous Charlie..."

"Most."

"Right. And about that *one* time you went tubing."

"Oh. Ha. Yeah, it's not that interesting."

"I'm sure you'll make it sound good."

Confidence beams from his eyes. Is it possible he hears me in a way I've never heard myself? It seems too far-fetched.

"Now," Mac says, looking at the house, "can we please get out of here?"

The walk back is silent and determined, both of us too cold to mumble more than a few words, and Mac chewing on the beef jerky he couldn't wait to bite into. My body moves with purpose while my mind splinters into fragments. I haven't even started making sense of all the interrelated pieces.

After a long battle with the elements, we make it back to where we started. The museum filled up with heat while we were gone, but it's not enough. I've never been this cold. Our brief indoor pit stops only made being outside more relentless. Now I'm wiggling to keep the blood from locking up inside of me.

"It's warmer in the back," I say.

I keep the lights off in the front room. Paranoia.

Before following, Mac removes his wool hat and stretches it over the head of the Edison bust. Those of us who work at the museum are used to politely scolding the thoughtless visitors who feel the need to touch things that are set behind protective rope and clearly marked DO NOT TOUCH. But I'm currently not working, and the absurdity of Thomas Edison wearing a beanie delights me. I may be delirious.

The back room is warmer, true, but barely. I notice Mac's bandage swinging loosely, its stickiness spoiled by our outdoor trek. He tears it off and sticks it audaciously to the wall.

"Is there a hand dryer in the bathroom?" Mac says, palming through his hat hair. "We could use it to dry our clothes."

"Fecal matter," I say.

"Um, no thanks."

"Those hand blowers are full of fecal matter."

He laughs.

"I'm serious," I say. "I heard it on NPR. All they do is blow feces around. You're better off letting your hands drip-dry."

"Wow. That is educational." He works up another plan. "We could take off our clothes and let them air-dry."

In the movies, a guy will say this type of thing to convince a girl to get naked. Is that what's happening here? Mac seems to be suggesting something as trivial to him as removing his shoes. I do not share this sense of bodily ease. I currently lag behind my girlfriends in this area. Isla has been felt up and has done her own feeling, and Brooke's already had sex (which is a secret I'm not supposed to share with Isla). Meanwhile, I still haven't open-mouth kissed a boy, let alone stripped in front of one.

"What are your clothes made of—cotton?" Mac says.

"I don't know."

"They call cotton the death fabric. This survival guy I watch says if you ever fall into frozen water, you have to get all the cotton off your body right away."

"I have no plans to fall into frozen water," I say.

"Do you have a better idea?"

My leggings (part cotton) have a darkened soak line above my frostbitten ankles. My mismatched socks (100% cotton) feel damp inside my wet canvas sneakers. (Why didn't I grab my UGGS?) Mac's coat has done a fine job protecting my red sweatshirt (soft, soft cotton). No, I do not have a better idea. I guess I'll just have to freeze to death.

We're practically running in place to shake off the cold.

"Too bad this room isn't big enough for suicides," Mac says.

I give him a look.

"It's what they make us do in soccer. You run to one line, run back, run to a farther line, run back. You keep going, farther and farther, always back to the start, basically until you're ready to kill yourself."

Those suicides. It's a cruel bit of wordplay, given the events of the night, but Mac appears oblivious to any double meaning. While I'm over here, nerves frayed, reading into everything Mac says and wondering if and how any of it leads back to the mistakes I've made, Mac has miraculously regained his lightness. He became darker and more serious the closer we got to his house and goofier and more playful again as we retreated.

"I know," Mac says, raising his fists in victory. "Push-ups."

I can't pinpoint why this unappealing suggestion comes off as endearing. Maybe it's how genuinely excited he looks and how genuinely excited he expects me to be. I am not excited. But it's the first idea he's had that I can at least entertain.

Mac removes the coat he's wearing. I take off only my hood and drop to my knees. I place my hands on the ground, assuming the position, and when I do, it hits me like a ton of snowy bricks: déjà vu.

It was this exact activity—push-ups—that started it all. The aftermath, specifically, is what inspired an Edison-like invention: my alter ego. What are the chances? I don't do a single push-up my whole life, practically, and when I finally do, it sets off a serious chain reaction.

Mac misinterprets my hesitation. His eyes focus on my lack of symmetry. I assume he feels pity and is going to let me off the hook, but he does the opposite.

"Come on," he says, like the team captain he probably is (or was). "Get after it."

He has no clue what's going on inside my head right now, but that's not his fault. He's treating me like an equal. It's what I always say I want.

I can do a push-up, just not well. I attempt my first one. It's not my limb difference impeding me; it's the puffy coat. Oh well. I'd rather do clumsy push-ups than shed a vital layer.

Meanwhile, Mac is up and down, up and down, again and again.

"Show-off," I say.

"I do this for a living."

Pride, or the hope of maintaining what little I have, keeps me going. I complete ten sad push-ups and call it quits.

"Do you feel warmer?" Mac says.

"I feel nauseous."

I sit up and wait for my breathing to return to normal.

My last set of push-ups was just a few months ago, but it feels like another lifetime. In a way, it was. Soon after I completed them, I was reborn as someone entirely new.

You're at the coffee shop across from school where people hang in the afternoon. Normally, you're not one of these people. But today your sluggish body craves a coffee and maybe a donut too.

Ahead of you in line are classmates Finley Wooten and Elena Gonzalez.

Ms. Millard is such a dick, Finley says. *Making her do it in front of everyone.*

I know, Elena says. *Poor girl.*

"Poor girl" is you. Earlier today in gym Ms. Millard selected you to demonstrate a proper push-up. (Naïvely, Ms. Millard was trying to empower you.) Finley and Elena were there to witness it. They don't realize you're standing behind them now.

I feel bad, Elena says.

Me too, Finley says. *I feel like she'd be super cute if it weren't for that.*

That.

I mean, she's still cute, Elena says.

Sure, but you know what I mean.

Yeah, no, I totally agree.

If ever there was a time to make yourself heard, it's now. This is the moment you've been waiting for to *not* be quiet. You search for the wittiest, most who-do-you-think-you-are response. The kind that people hear and immediately stop what they're doing and slow clap because you stood up for what counts, you delivered the kind of justice that everyone craves.

Your mind goes blank. Your lips are glued shut. Your ears doubt what they heard. You wimp out. You say nothing. Quietly, you leave.

But what they said—it never leaves you.

Days later, Finley Wooten, the girl who thinks you'd actually be pretty if you weren't so ugly, posts a selfie. Ever since the coffee shop, you've been stalking Finley at school and online. Stewing over what she said. Obsessing about what you *should* have said. (You're less concerned with Elena. She's just a follower.)

In her selfie Finley appears in semi-profile, hair in a bun, neck exposed. You notice something. Something you've noticed before.

Before your mind can resist, your mismatched thumbs act in solidarity to type a comment:

> I love your technique, Fin. How you always keep the tag on new clothes so you can wear something only once and return it. Great way to give the impression of a never-repeating wardrobe. Perfect for anyone on a tight budget. Thanks for the tip!

The reaction is quick and intense. Emojis of shocked faces, laughing tears, hands over mouths. Responses to your response:

> Ouch

> OMG. Never noticed that.

> Gotta hide the tag better girl!

> Oh no. This means war.

Suddenly, We're All Gonna Die, the account you're using when you leave the comment, has thirty-eight new followers, more trickling in by the minute. What does it mean? It means they hear you. They support you. They agree with you. A follow is a way of saying all of this without having to say any of it. They don't want Finley Wooten making problems for *them*. Neither do you, actually. You quickly close the WAGD account before anyone can identify the person behind the comment.

Finley takes down the photo. What a rush! Part panic, part exhilaration. Did that just happen? Your friends hypothesize about who was running the WAGD account. None of them suspect it's you, even though you told them all about the incident with Finley at the coffee shop. You want to take credit for putting Finley in her place, but something keeps you quiet.

Maybe this is what you were born to do. Maybe this is your superpower. What does Neel always say? *Eyes of god*, he says. *You're like the eyes of god*. The way you spot the details he misses. Mom calls you a hawk. You learned it from Dad.

When you were nine, you attended one of Dad's classes. On Take Your Child to Work Day. A big lecture hall. It was boring, listening to him drone on about Shakespeare.

A few students were late to class. Dad glanced down at his thick silver watch and went back to teaching. Another student came in, and this time Dad said, *Welcome, Mr. Ratner.* You wondered whether the kid was important. Why else would Dad announce his arrival? Because moments later two more students arrived, and Dad just glanced at his watch and kept teaching.

After class, Dad took you to lunch at the student center. He ate a salad and you had egg rolls and fried rice. You asked him why he called out the one kid and nobody else.

Good ears, Dad said.

He explained that Andrew Ratner, a freshman, was a bright kid, a good kid, he just needed extra attention. At first, Dad ignored his tardiness. But Andrew found other ways to make his presence known: cracking his knuckles, talking to peers, falling asleep. Dad would sometimes even pass Andrew on his way into the building, and he began to wonder whether Andrew was purposely waiting until after Dad had begun teaching to come to class. The next time Andrew was late, Dad called him out. He didn't like doing it. It was a distraction to the other students.

But, Dad said, in between bites of snappy lettuce, *after I gave Andrew his own special introduction, I had zero problems. For a while, at least. Every few classes I have to remind him that I see him. We do this little dance, he and I. That's okay. Every kid needs something different. Adults are the same way. There's a way in to every person. You just have to discover what it is.*

What's the way in to Mom?

He smiles. *That's easy. Back rubs. Absolute best way to soften her up.*

And what's the way in to me?

You? You're a "show me" kind of person. A natural doubter. You don't believe it until you see it. I can tell you I love you a hundred times, and you'll shrug me off, roll your eyes. But then I give you one long hug, just hold you there, and you're putty in my hands. You just melt.

You've never thought about this before, but now that he's saying it, you realize he's right.

You tell him that you know his way in. It's books. If you ask him for a toy or a tablet, he'll always say no. But if you ask him for a book, the answer is always yes.

He stops chewing. *Uh-oh*, he says. *I think I created a monster.*

Dad,

I don't know how you're always so patient with everyone. I can't stand how some people are. How they behave. I don't know how to not let it bother me. Sometimes I feel like I'm going to explode.

Love,
Tegan

Tegan,

Don't explode.

Love,
Dad

4:46 PM

When I got downstairs, Charlie had already left the house and the kitchen looked like a war zone. Cabinets were open. A jar lay sideways spilling a mystery spice on the counter. The faucet ran unattended while Mom dug through the fridge. Charlie makes it look easy when he cooks, which is basically every night. He'll make Mom and me something to eat before taking off for his shift. When not performing at weddings, he works nights as a sanitation worker.

I shut off the faucet. Mom looked up. "Oh, hi," she said, a little embarrassed. "It's been so long since I've done this."

It had been.

Over the sink was a hanging pothos. The soil felt dry. I filled the watering can and soaked the pothos and the other plants. Five in the kitchen alone.

I sat down at the table. Mom placed a cutting board full of carrots in front of me. "Can you chop these, please?"

Please, thank you, sorry—she's like a midwesterner who's

only pretending to have been born and raised in New Jersey. She was practically predestined to be a preschool teacher.

I lifted the knife and got to work.

A moistness announced itself. I looked up and saw Mom struggling to disrobe a whole chicken from its plastic packaging, her bare hands squeezing the raw body, sending invisible droplets of salmonella god knows where.

"You know I don't eat meat, right?" I said, because now seemed like the right time.

She whipped her head around. The naked chicken was suspended in the air with nowhere to go. "Oh my god. I'm so sorry. Of course I know that. I was just trying to make something you liked."

She placed the chicken in a pot, washed her hands, and paused at the counter. Her can-do spirit was now can-not. Because of me.

The truth was that upstairs in my room, I had been thinking I kind of wanted the soup. It had been so long. I'd eat just the plain broth. I'm not the strictest vegetarian, anyway. But that was before I saw the poor naked bird being groped like that.

Mom wasn't sure how to proceed.

"You can still make it," I told her, taking hold of a fresh carrot, as if to emphasize for both of us the vegetable presence in the meal.

She filled the pot with water and put it on a burner before sitting next to me at the table. It felt a little too close.

"How are you?" she said.

I remembered a meeting with the school guidance counselor a few years ago that began the same way.

"Fine," I said now, trying to make it sound like the obvious truth.

"Everything okay with you and Neel?"

I hadn't told her anything about what had happened at the mall, but she'd gathered enough clues to form a realistic picture. My mood on the way home was far different from what it had been when we'd left the house hours prior.

"We're good," I said.

"What about Isla and Brooke? They haven't been over in so long."

Even worse than not having Charlie here to cook was not having him here to keep my mom from having the time and space to grill me.

"Isla's been busy with theater. Brooke is Brooke. She comes and goes, depending on what guy she's into at the moment. We eat lunch together most days. It's not like I don't see them."

She nodded one too many times.

"What?" I said.

"I'm just asking. I don't know. You seem..."

The way she talks sometimes, tiptoeing as if I'm so breakable. Or it's like fishing, casting a line in every direction until I finally bite. I wasn't biting.

"You seem a little distant lately. I get the sense you're feeling all these things, but you never say what they are."

"You have no idea what I'm feeling."

"That's why I'm asking."

"You're assuming."

Her hand fell to the table, reaching, but not fully. "If there's something you're holding in and you want to talk…"

I was holding everything in—every single thing.

"I'm not holding anything in," I said.

"Tegan."

I pushed back my chair. "What, Mom?"

She calibrated her voice, a real professional. "I know that's not true."

It made me laugh. "What do you know? What do you *think* you know?"

She breathed in, inhaling all the air available to her. "I can never say the right thing."

"Just say what you want to say, Mom. Is that so hard? What now? I haven't been late to homeroom once since the last time. I finished my essay for English like I said I would. I told you I'd start babysitting again if you really want me to. I don't get it. What else do you want from me?"

"I know you email your father."

It felt like I'd been dunked inside the burning pot of water.

"You went into my computer," I said.

"No," she insisted.

"If I wanted you to know, I would have told you. But I didn't, did I?"

"It was an accident. I wasn't trying to pry."

I was up from my chair, boiling over. "You are such a bad liar."

"Tegan, if I wanted to lie to you, I wouldn't have brought it up. I would have just pretended I didn't know."

She waited for me to think it through, but I didn't care how rational or convincing she sounded. I didn't believe any of it.

"I know what this is about," I said. "I know. You can't stand that I'd rather talk to *him* than you."

She remained seated. She didn't feel like fighting. Honestly, neither did I.

"I didn't do anything wrong," I said. Saying it unglued a part of me that was barely held together.

She heard my ungluing, moms and their ears, and she tried to come to me. "I didn't say you did. That's not what this is about. I'm just trying to check in with you, that's all."

"I can't," I said, retreating to the hall.

"Where are you going?"

I reached the foot of the stairs and stopped. There was no hiding up there.

"I can't be here."

"What do you mean?" she said, following me.

"There's nowhere for me to be."

By the front door, a pile of shoes. My feet dived into stiff canvas.

Mom arrived. "Stop this. We're having dinner."

"I'm not hungry."

The door opened and the cold rushed in.

"You're not leaving this house."

She tried to take hold of me, but I was already out.

"This is insane, Tegan. Walking around in this. Why do you have to be this way?"

I turned on the walkway.

"I just wanted to talk to him. Is that so bad? Why'd you have to ruin that?"

Under the porch light, arms crossed, she had no answer.

So I went, and I didn't look back.

After tonight's earlier failed attempt at dinner, I'm finally sitting down to eat. Mac and I are on the floor in the back room. It's quite a spread, the best worst food I've ever seen. Mom's hot soup would really be the cure for my icy bones right now, but that's obviously not an option. This convenience store supper is warming up my soul just fine.

"You live in that white house on the corner of Becker, right?" Mac says.

Registering my shock, he explains, "I used to be friends with Blake."

"Right, Blake Lewis," I confirm. "He lived next door. His family moved to Texas."

"This was in, like, third grade. I just remember he had one of those huge arcade basketball games in his basement."

Mac waits for me to agree, even though I was never in Blake's house, let alone his basement. Still, I nod like I know.

I sit cross-legged while he stretches his legs out wide, the mouth of Pac-Man ready to gobble me up, except there's ample space between us. Having already wolfed down his first energy bar, he tears the wrapper off the second with oblivious ease. I usually have to break into snack bags with my teeth or a set of keys. Tonight a pair of museum scissors was my ladylike tool of choice.

"You got any siblings?" Mac says.

It seems his mind is still on his brother. Why else would he ask me this question?

"Only child," I say.

"Look out."

"What? I can get along with others."

There's doubt in his smile. "Which others?"

I start naming people—"Isla Sheppard, Brooke Mandelbaum"—until I realize he was only teasing and never expected me to start listing my friends one by one. I feel extra shame knowing how withdrawn I've become with my oldest friends these past few months—my fault, but also theirs.

"I see you with that guy. Neel, right?"

It's starting to get weird how much Mac seems to know about me.

"Is he your boyfriend?" Mac asks.

Frappuccino dribbles down my lips. "My *boyfriend*? Neel Singh?"

I'm flattered that Mac thinks I have a boyfriend and a little insulted that he believes it's Neel. It's not that Neel is ugly, far from it (he's got thick, lustrous hair that most girls would kill for); it's just that he's Neel.

"He's just a good friend," I say, laughing it off.

Those words—*just* and *good*—feel like betrayals. *Just*

95

makes it seem like I don't really care about Neel, and *good* is a downgrade from *best*.

Isla and Brooke have wondered the same thing about me and Neel. I guess the two of us being in a secret romance together is the only explanation they can come up with for why I might choose to hang out with him over them. Their lack of insight about the situation is part of the problem. But anyway.

Does it mean something that Mac is curious about my relationship status? He's such a skilled conversationalist, moving effortlessly from one topic to the next, that it's hard to know what to make of any one thing he says.

He seems to be gearing up now for another question as he sips a protein shake. I'm starting to wonder whether this is strategic: If he's the one always asking the questions, he never has to answer any.

"I think it's my turn," I say.

He wipes his lips. "Go for it."

I have so many questions to ask Mac Durant. I should start small, but I already know where he lives, that he has one sibling, and that he works at Sneaker World. I guess I could ask him—not that it's consuming me or anything—but I could ask whether he's seeing anyone. That wouldn't be outrageously presumptuous and random, given that he just asked me a similar question, right? I mean, I'm only curious, since we're talking.

But there's a more pressing question in my brain. "Are you like this with everyone?"

He pushes aside his empty food wrappers, finally satiated. "Am I like what?"

"I don't know. You just seem..." I already started, so I guess I have to say it. "Before tonight, I honestly didn't think you knew who I was."

He stares at me. A driver's license would list his eyes as brown, but only because there's no shorthand for the color they produce, this warm, sun-beaming gold.

"I know who you are," Mac says.

I shove a whole Oreo into my mouth. A theory that I had been avoiding all night announces itself: Is it possible his arrival tonight was not a coincidence? Did he *mean* to find me here?

"Last year there was an assembly," Mac says, pushing his sleeve up and scratching his forearm. "Some motivational speaker guy came and gave a talk. You remember him? He wore a bow tie."

"Right," I say, nervous about where this is going.

"He was talking about this kid who jumped off a bridge. He said maybe it could've ended differently if the people in his life reached out. I looked around, and it seemed like no one was listening. People were on their phones or making jokes. The guy was pretty goofy, but I was trying to hear him out, and I felt like I was the only one. Until I looked across the gym and saw you."

"Me?"

He confirms with one slow nod.

I wipe cookie crumbs from my lips.

"I just remember your eyes were glued to the guy. Like, what he was saying mattered to you. Maybe it didn't, I don't know—but the way you looked, it sort of matched how I was feeling in that moment."

I remember the assembly and even where I was sitting. At some point, I probably noticed Mac on the opposite bleachers, but I have no specific memory of seeing him. The fact that Mac was across the way noticing *me* and that he could sense even a little bit of what I was feeling is absolutely ludicrous. It's true the speaker's story had connected with me. Not in a dangerous, life-or-death way. It left me feeling disconnected and lonely—surrounded by hundreds of people but anonymous, unseen. Turns out, in that very moment, I was literally being seen.

Mac runs his fingers through his messy hair, messing it up even more. Not in that self-aware way guys do. He doesn't care about what his hands or his hair is doing. His mind is preoccupied.

"There's so much superficial shit going on at school. I just don't have time for it," Mac says.

I nod in a natural and not-at-all-anxious way. "I know what you mean."

His eyes won't let me go. "I thought you might."

The horror: I assumed he was shallow, and meanwhile he saw the depth in me. I grab another Oreo and twist off the top.

"Hand me one of those, will you?" Mac says, stretching closer.

I throw him a cookie instead. He catches it easily, as if

there's nothing I could throw at him that he wouldn't accept. But I can't tell what, if anything, truly penetrates his surface.

I ask him, "What's your way in?"

He shoves the whole cookie in his mouth. "My *way in?*"

"Yeah. Your weak spot. Your Achilles' heel. If someone wants to win you over, what do they have to do?"

His full cheeks need time to make room. He gives the question serious thought.

"Just be honest," Mac says. "That's it, really. Anything fake, I can't stand." He reaches for the bottle that he brought from home. It's been waiting ominously by his side this whole time. "That's sort of why I ended up here."

He twists the cap off the bottle, and the motion twists my insides.

A quick sniff. He tilts back his head and swallows. He looks horrified as he extends the bottle to me.

"You're not making me want to try it," I say, accepting the torch.

His voice gets caught in his throat. "It's rough. I'm not going to lie."

The label reads SMIRNOFF. It's vodka. I feel weird drinking when I already sense where this is going, but I also know that I won't be able to get through it without a little numbing. I blow out air, a deep-sea diver going down. A rushed, big gulp, and I'm coughing.

Mac laughs with compassion. "You all right?"

I insist that I am, even though I can tell my face has turned as red as my sweatshirt. I've only drunk vodka mixed with soda (at Isla's once; her parents pretended not to know).

Recovering feebly, I offer my verdict: "It's delicious."

I give him back the bottle. He feels its weight. "I don't really drink," he says. His glee fades, jaw tightens. A fog sets in, that same darkness he arrived with tonight and seems to only temporarily keep at bay.

He brings his knees in, the heels of his shoes kissing the floor. A curling up. It creates more space between us, but I suddenly feel crowded in.

"My mom was supposed to pick me up from work, but my dad showed up instead."

Hearing this, I wish I hadn't given up the bottle just yet. I may need more numbing. Like, immediately.

"In my house, any sudden change of plans is bad news," Mac continues. "They had a fight, I guess. My mom left and went to stay at my aunt's."

He pauses, perhaps wondering whether he should stop before he begins. His arms dangle over his knees, his fingers strangling the bottle's neck. He checks my face, and whatever he sees convinces him to go on.

"Ever since my brother left for college back in the fall, things have gone to shit. He started drinking again, my dad. He had quit for a few years."

He brings the bottle up and hovers his nose over its top.

"I could tell from the smell coming off him. Even before I got in the car, I knew. The way he meant to unlock the door but lowered the window instead. How the radio was too loud."

Mac lowers the bottle to the floor but keeps it in his grasp.

"He started driving and I heard a sound, something dragging on the road. In the mirror I could see snow shooting up behind us. I asked him what it was and he shrugged it off. We got to the house and I saw the mailbox, what was left of it. He didn't say a word, just pulled us into the garage. I got out and saw this big dent in the bumper where he must have backed over the mailbox. I started cleaning it up. I didn't know what else to do. Meanwhile, he's in the driver's seat, engine running, blasting some song he loves, not a care in the world."

Mac stares into the clear bottle, seeing things, but not quite feeling them. He doesn't look like he needs a drink to be numb.

"Then the garage door starts coming down and I'm thinking, great, he's going to get himself killed."

He breaks for a time, leaving me to sit with that image, his father's fate in the balance, at risk of carbon monoxide poisoning.

He takes a second drink. This one goes down smoother. He passes me the bottle. I wait before drinking, unsure whether I deserve to blunt the sting of what Mac is revealing.

"It's been building for months. Back in the fall, there was this one night..."

I go ahead and take the drink.

"My team finished in second place. Coach took us all out for dinner to the Cheesecake Factory. We spread out over a few tables. At some point I look over and there's my dad, seated at the bar. He wasn't supposed to be there. He had been at the game that afternoon, and I'd already said I was getting a lift and would see him at home. He must have found out that some of the other parents were planning to hang at the restaurant until we finished. But he wasn't with the other parents.

He was by himself at the bar. There was nothing I could really do about it. I just tried to ignore him.

"Near the end of the meal, we heard this loud crash. Our goalie points to the bar: 'Bro, is that your dad?' He was lying on the floor, flat on his back, the barstool knocked sideways. Coach told the team to sit down and finish eating. I went over to help. Another parent offered to drive him home, but I called a car instead. I felt like I should go with him, so I missed the end of the dinner. My mom had to bring him back for his car the next day."

I'm certain now that I don't deserve any dulling of the pain, but I drink more anyway, and when I'm finished, I push the bottle as far away as it'll go.

He leaves it where it is. He brings his knees in tighter.

"It's the same shit my brother was dealing with for years, but I was clueless about it. I sort of knew, but I didn't really know. I was spared somehow. I guess just from James being there."

This last bit feels new even to Mac, a discovery in the moment. He stares into space, conjuring images I can't see.

"Then there's the fakeness," Mac says. "I'm trying to help my dad off the floor of a restaurant and one of my teammates is sitting there fucking filming it and the video gets sent around. I don't know who did it, but someone knows. Now I'm supposed to get on the field with these guys? Not going to happen. I had to quit. I had no choice."

Mac shakes his head, still trying to make sense of it. "Anyway, I'm guessing you saw the video."

I remain quiet.

"Seems like everyone did," Mac says, resigned to the fact. "It got posted by Nightshade and spread from there."

He looks at me a second time. He's bared his soul and he needs me to say something.

"Yeah," I tell him, sinking through the floor. "I think I heard about that."

You don't want to hurt people. You just want fairness. Unfairness is the natural way, one person born like this, the rest born like that. One parent is here, the other... And so, fairness is a job that humanity takes on. That you take on.

You're focused on the Finley Wootens of the world. The elite. The privileged. The coasters. The ones who get all the attention and don't deserve it. Those blessed with too much this or that—resources, ability, luck. The popular, pimple-free, fit, cocky, joyful, comfortable, protected, applauded, desired, gifted. Whatever they are, the rest of us are not. And that's not cool. Not anymore. And they should know it—that it's not cool anymore.

You go after them one by one, the same way you went after Finley. You're still on a wild high after taking her down, not hesitating, just typing, typing, typing. Using the new anonymous account you created for this sole purpose, you call out all the fakeness, arrogance, and hypocrisy you see around you. Like how the self-righteous environmentalist grabs the hugest stack of napkins at lunch and tosses most of them unused in the garbage. (Not even in the recycling can!) Or how snooty fashionista Ana's recent passion for long dresses might have something to do with getting her name tattooed in cursive on her calf and the long rising swoop after the second *a* looking awfully similar to the letter *l*. Or how the principal's saintlike pet vapes every day with the custodian behind the computer lab between fourth and fifth periods.

Nightshade is a private account. Your profile pic is a LEGO knight figure. There are no posts on your page. You're commenting on what other people post. You don't create content; you destroy it.

And shockingly well. At school you hear people react to your commentary. On social media, they discuss it like the new season of a popular series.

Nightshade strikes again!

Has to be a student. The things they know.

Definitely. I have my guesses.

This person is evil.

Relax. It's harmless.

Harmless? Are you crazy? This is wrong! It's harassment!

I know I shouldn't laugh, but it's hard not to.

You wouldn't if it was about you.

Anyone else paranoid they'll be next?

Totally! Second guessing everything I post!

I'd be honored to get the shade.

Don't encourage this loser.

Too late.

I don't think I've ever hated someone so much in my entire life.

Same.

I disagree. This guy's a genius.

Amen!

The stir you've created makes you nervous. Proud, too, honestly, because you're not only affecting what people talk about, but how they behave. In public, at least. The environmentalist stops wasting napkins. The principal's pet curbs his vaping. Still, did you go too far? Years of pent-up hurt and frustration burst out in a firestorm of verbal fury. You just couldn't hold it in any longer.

People send threatening messages to your account. What surprises you is that the majority of the hate you receive isn't even aimed at you. These messages are from people who have hurtful things they want to say about *other* people, and they want you to say it so they don't have to. You've tapped into something. Touched a nerve. At first you ignore these requests. You want no part of them. You've gone far enough. But something gnaws at you. A deep craving rising to the surface. Quiet for so long, you now have a voice, and people are asking you to use it. Why deny them? Why deny yourself?

Using secret information you receive from another person, Nightshade, for the first time, posts a story.

Turns out self-proclaimed influencer Wendy Joyce Lee purchased ten thousand of her twelve thousand followers. Behold: the literal receipt.

Within a few short hours, your followers double. Then triple. Unlike Wendy Joyce Lee, you've earned your followers, every single one. Your story is reposted dozens of times. It's all anyone is talking about: Nightshade.

What if you kept it going a little while longer? What if you refused to stay silent? Not only for you—for everyone messaging you. They feel silenced, too. You could be their voice. A conduit for all their pain—the jealousy, the bitterness, the rage.

More stories come.

> That rumor everyone takes as gospel about "tough guy" Victor Trokic being in a gang? Victor started it himself so no one would mess with him.

> Since when does Karen Lockhart run track? It could be this doctored photo is what got her that scholarship to Princeton.

> The reason Ezra Rosen always has weed is because his uncle works for a Mexican drug cartel.

There's an energy around you, around your account. You feel it in the halls, in class, on the bus. This buzz you've created. Ah, to be heard, finally. Is there anything better?

After twenty-four hours, the stories vanish into the ether, unless others repost them, which they often do. It's no longer about how you feel. It's about how *they* feel. You're just a messenger.

It's one of these messages from a stranger that puts you in the predicament you're in now. You receive a video. You play it. In a busy restaurant, a middle-aged man is sprawled on the floor. A young guy in a tracksuit enters the frame. Along with the bartender, he helps the man to his feet. The man can barely stand, but he reaches for his drink on the bar and finishes it before stumbling off-screen. The video cuts off. You're not sure what to make of it until you see the message it came with: *Mac Durant at the Cheesecake Factory with his drunk dad.*

The message is from a private account and an unfamiliar tag. It's proof of what everyone's been whispering about for years. A huge score for Nightshade. *If* you post it. But should you? This is Mac Durant you're talking about. He's like a mystical being, untouchable.

Untouchable. The word flips in your mind. From one exalted to one ignored. Untouchable is you. To all of them, including Mac Durant. He's never once acknowledged your existence. Why should he be spared? Isn't he the embodiment of elite and privileged?

You write a caption to go along with the video:

> Yup, Mac Durant's dad definitely has a drinking problem.
> I guess Mr. Perfect's life isn't so perfect after all.

You post it and move on.

I 'm sorry," I say.

Mac stands, stretches his legs. "Don't be sorry. You didn't do anything."

How wrong he is. I want to say it again and again, *I'm sorry, I'm sorry, I'm sorry,* but saying it a thousand times won't fix what I've done.

Nightshade is no longer active. It hasn't been for weeks. I don't post or comment anymore, and I never will again. Even so, it's been impossible to put it behind me. The account still exists. Messages still come in. People still talk about it—obviously.

I feel sick. My stomach is a nauseated swirl of Oreos, vodka, and regret. The painful mix expands in my gut once it hits me that Nightshade is the reason Mac isn't on a team anymore. I can't even look at him, which I'm now realizing is not only insensitive after everything he's told me but also a little suspicious.

"So that's the story," I say, peeking up at him, trying to appear normal.

He meets my eyes, staring hard. I've learned to live daily with the fear that my double life will be revealed. I'm always waiting and never ready.

"It's a lot, I know," Mac says.

He looks away, and I realize in his new shyness that my fears are just fears: He has no clue I was the one who posted the video. How could it have been? *Why* would it have been?

"It is a lot," I say.

He turns and gazes at me. It feels unbearable, my secret.

But would it help him right now if he knew? Or would bringing it up only take the burden off me and drop it on Mac? He just went through a major event with his dad, and the last thing I want is to add more drama on top of that.

"But I'm glad," I say. "That you told me."

He exhales, shoulders sloping, face relaxing. A kind of relief sets in. For both of us.

I promised myself I'd go with it, and it's time I got back on track with that plan. *Our* plan. Mac is here and so am I. The outside world is just noise. I'm ready for more vodka.

I stand up and realize that more vodka will not be necessary. It's finally hitting me, all the shots I took. How many was it? Actually, I don't feel half bad. Dare I say, I feel kind of hopeful.

Thankfully, Mac seems ready to move on from the subject of his dad. I want the playful Mac back. Enough of this heaviness. He's fiddling with one of our hands-on exhibits. Patrons are actually encouraged to touch these gadgets. I point out one machine in particular.

"You want to see something cool?" I say.

I pull open a thin drawer and grab a scrap of paper. I twist the paper into a stick. The machine has a pencil-sharpener-looking mechanism, and when you turn it, a wire lights up. I press the paper to the wire while spinning the wheel.

"There's a candle on the ledge," I say. "Grab it."

Mac springs into action and gets the candle.

"We're going to set fire to this paper and then use it to light the candle."

"You're like that survival guy I was telling you about," Mac says.

"The guy who made me terrified of cotton?"

"Yeah, that guy. Instead of rocks and sticks, you've got... whatever this is."

"I like science." As soon as the words leave my mouth, I realize how cringeworthy they are. Also untrue. "I guess what I like, actually, are inventions."

The paper starts to smoke. Mac readies the candle.

"There's this fair coming up," I say. "The inventors fair. They do it every year around Edison's birthday, February eleventh. I'm sure you've never been."

Mac reacts as if I've just slandered him. I guess I don't realize how I sound sometimes, how much edge there is in my voice.

"I just mean you're probably busy, that's all," I say.

The paper catches fire. I press it to the wick of the candle that Mac is holding, and soon the candle lights.

"Cool," Mac says, moderately impressed.

I blow out the candle and return it to its spot. "Neel and I were thinking about submitting an invention for this year's fair. I had an idea, and he's been trying to work out the details. It's pretty ambitious. That's what Neel tells me. Apparently these competitions are mostly automatic dog feeders and stuff like that, you know. But my idea is kind of *not* that." I pause for air. "You want to hear what it is?"

Mac stops spinning the pencil-sharpener wheel he's been testing.

I hold out my right hand. "Can I see your phone?"

He removes it from his pocket and realizes that it's not turning on. "Shit," Mac says. "It's dead."

"It doesn't matter." I grab it and place my pointer finger on the screen. "Every time we put our fingers to the screen, we create electricity," I say, repeating a fact I learned from Neel. "Our phones react in different ways depending on *how* we touch it. So the screen might shake or vibrate or click, whatever. It can give us the sensation that we're actually pressing down on a real button. All this technology already exists."

I return his phone and reach for my half-eaten licorice package on the floor. "Okay, now I have my phone here and you have yours there. Let's say we each have our fingers on our screens." Mac plays along, positioning his finger on his real phone, and I do the same on my licorice phone. "So, here's my idea. What if"—pausing for suspense—"when you press down on *your* screen, I feel it on *mine*? I actually *feel you*."

I wait for his reaction.

"Why do we need the phones?" Mac says. "Why can't we just touch for real?"

"We can't. We're not in the same place."

"We're not? I thought we were."

"No, you're at your house and I'm at mine. We're living our own separate lives."

"Oh. Okay," Mac says.

He doesn't get it. How could he? He doesn't know how important a touch screen is for someone like me. He's never struggled to work a bulky game controller or tried to clumsily peck at a traditional keyboard.

His lack of enthusiasm doesn't get me down—too much. I've got vodka confidence. "Someone's going to invent it," I say, full of unusual faith. "It might not be me and Neel, but mark my words, one day it'll be a reality. People touching each other without even touching."

Mac crosses his arms and ponders. "What are your grades like?"

I snort—by accident. "Not great."

"I don't believe it."

"Neel is the tech genius. I just had the idea."

"I'm not talking about that. You're obviously smart."

This makes me blush.

I've been tested for ADD, dyscalculia, auditory processing disorder, you name it. The doctors say there's nothing wrong with me. One therapist I met with believed the reason I was having difficulty at school was obvious. But I wasn't ready to talk about *that*.

"It's hard for me to focus sometimes," I say, which is true, but apparently not a medical concern—just a parental one. "Let me guess, you get straight As."

He leans against the wall, head resting back. "Flattered, thanks, but no. More like solid Bs."

That checks out, actually. He mentioned wanting to get his grades up for college.

"You remember in seventh grade, in our English class, when we got partnered up?" I say.

The funny look on his face means he doesn't remember. How could I be so stupid to blurt that out?

"Vaguely," Mac says.

"It's fine," I say, not wanting his pity. "Don't say you remember if you don't."

"Well, can you be more specific?"

I inspect his face and find honest curiosity. I step, once more, out on a ledge. "We had to act out a scene together from *The Outsiders*."

I thought I was going to die, being that close to him, having to speak words that actually made sense. Luckily, Mac had the bigger part and did most of the talking.

It's clear from his extended silence that he has no recollection of this moment.

"I'm such an idiot," I say.

"Stop it," Mac says, laughing at what he feels is a silly matter.

"Let me ask you this. Were we both in Ms. Picerno's class in fourth grade?"

"Is this a trick question?"

"Just answer."

"Yes," Mac says with certainty.

"No. *You* had Ms. Picerno and I had Ms. Katz."

He's loving this, laughing at my expense. "Oh, come on. I don't remember stuff like that."

I'm a little hurt. It's all so clear in my mind. Our classrooms were next to each other, and everybody would pile into one room for holiday parties and the occasional movie. I remember Mac's class had a pet bird, white with a splash of orange. I remember that Ms. Picerno once sent Eric Adamo from our class to the principal for calling her Miss Piss (not to her face, but not quietly, either). And of course I remember how a month into the year the girl with the purple glasses switched from Mac's class to ours and the only available desk happened to be next to mine. Her name was Brooke and she told me she was a vegetarian. I thought that sounded pretty cool.

"You're not the first person to tell me I don't remember things," Mac says, only the faintest hint of laughter remaining in his cheeks. "People seem to remember the past so well. I feel bad that I don't. I don't remember a lot of my childhood."

He's gone serious again, and it's my fault. "You're still a child, you know. Technically."

He thinks about it. "Yeah," he says, but with deep reluctance, as if he can't stomach taking a win on a mere technicality. He's a contradiction: He sees his childhood as distant and done, but so many of his strongest qualities are that of a child. His sense of wonder. His naïve confidence. His restless energy. His bottomless hunger. Earlier tonight, when he barged in unwelcomed, his childlike way irritated me. Now I can't wait for it to reappear.

He steps closer to a photo on the wall. "I was too in my own head. I'm still like that. I look at people, I talk to them, but I'm not actually looking at them. I'm not really talking. I'm not even there most of the time. It's hard to actually be there."

I guess he's saying this so I don't take it personally that I mean nothing to him. It's not working as intended.

"You seem to remember some things," I say, trying to make sense of the times tonight when he *did* recall noticing me, including that one very specific time at the assembly.

"Yeah," Mac says. "It's like I remember the things I want to forget and forget the things I wish I could remember."

I repeat this in my mind and test it against my own life: It's a perfect fit.

Mac massages his neck. He grimaces as he applies pressure. It seems we can laugh all we want, but there's always a lingering pain below the surface that can't be ignored.

I walk over and clap loudly in his face.

He leans back, startled. "What was *that*?"

"You're being weird," I say, even though I don't know him well enough to know what's weird and what's not. I just don't want to feel like I'm here alone, like he knows something I don't (when really it's the opposite). I sense my newfound courage slipping away. "You can leave anytime you want," I say.

He shuts his eyes.

"I was thinking how nice it feels to have a space. Just somewhere to be, where I can take a moment."

A peaceful grin forms on his face.

"I feel like this is our house or something," Mac says. "Like we live here."

His eyes open. A blast of his golden glow.

"So no," Mac says. "I'm not ready to leave."

I scan the shelf that holds the museum's music collection. "How about a cylinder?"

Mac's eyebrows arch in suspicion, like I just offered him a trendy new narcotic. Nope. Vodka was plenty for me. A cylinder is neither illicit nor cutting edge.

"It's what music was recorded on before discs," I explain. "This one is from 1910."

I switch on our cylinder player, and the black tube (made of actual beeswax) begins to spin. A hiss leaks out of the horn and soon the record plays. The music feels squeezed and small, but the instrumentation is lush and expansive.

"What's this one called?" Mac asks.

"'By the Light of the Silvery Moon.'" It's the third song we've sampled so far.

I take a seat next to him along the wall. I keep landing a little closer to him every time I return from cueing up a new recording. At first, the proximity was accidental. At first.

"Of all his inventions, capturing sound has to be the coolest," Mac says.

"And he was basically deaf."

"Even cooler."

"I'm not joking," I say, because when I tell this to the average patron, they never believe I'm serious. "To hear the music his artists were recording, he'd lay his head against the horn and feel the vibrations."

"That's dedication."

"Or arrogance. He was super controlling."

"You don't cut a dude a break, do you?"

"Don't start with me again."

He tries to subdue a smile.

The moment Mac described the museum as our house, I swear a physical door opened before me and I saw Mac standing there, waiting inside, and I stepped through the doorway into the house, took off Mac's coat, finally, and here I am—home. I've always had that feeling about this place. In some ways, it feels more like home than home feels like home. And now Mac is with me and it's as though *he* belongs here too.

He holds up the bottle that used to contain his energy drink but has since been refilled at the bathroom sink. "More water?"

Oh yeah, that. I've been drinking a lot of water. Mac's suggestion. Maybe it's an athlete thing? Anyway, sure, let's be sensible and stay hydrated. "Yes, please."

He tops me off.

The song, only ninety seconds long, ends before Mac has had a chance to fully appreciate it. He asks me to play it a second time. I sigh. I really don't want to get up again.

"I'd do it myself but I'm afraid of getting yelled at," Mac says.

Fair point. I get up and reset the cylinder. The music crackles to life.

"You want to know something else?" I say, sliding back onto the floor. "He loved milk."

"Smart. Milk is delicious."

"Strongly disagree. Edison was drinking an insane amount of it. Like, instead of eating meals, he'd just drink milk all day. This guy, this *genius*, quotation marks, you see what I'm doing there, he believed milk was a cure for major diseases. What is that?"

"I'm imagining Thomas Edison being alive today and you're, like, sending him angry tweets."

"No, I prefer to just vent to you."

"Lucky me."

He glances over.

The museum features a number of magnets, each on display to demonstrate the power of electric currents, but the one staring back at me now with its golden shimmer has more pull than all of them combined. I can't resist. My neck extends, mouth opening, head floating, but it's too far—I stop short, and I bite down on his shoulder.

A hiss as the song ends.

My teeth unclench and I sit up. His jaw hangs open, total shock. Any pain he feels from my sudden shoulder attack he keeps inaudible.

"You bit me," Mac says, eyes enormous.

I did. "Is that cotton?" I say, referring to his shirt. "It's delicious."

I stand up, pretending as though it's no big deal for one person to take a small chomp of another. As I return to the player, I deftly move the conversation along. "I feel like we need to hear that song a third time. You were yapping through it."

Still recovering from my attempt at cannibalism, Mac accepts the lie I've just told.

I cue up the cylinder, and on my way back to the floor, I refuse to look at him. I shut my eyes for full concentration.

> By the light of the silvery moon,
> I want to spoon.
> To my honey I'll croon love's tune.
> Honeymoon, keep a-shining in June,
> Your silvery beams will bring love dreams.
> We'll be cuddling soon,
> by the silvery moon.

When it ends, I look over. Mac's eyes are closed. I wait for him to speak first.

"My dad will stop at every flea market, every garage sale, looking for records. He was into vinyl before it was cool again. He was never *not* into it."

While I'm over here trying to find creative ways of ignoring the obvious ocean between us, Mac just dives right in.

"My mom hates the smell of old records, so she made him move all his stuff down to the basement."

That cozy feeling of home fades as I think back to peering

around the curtain in Mac's basement, into his father's listening area.

"I feel like he'd like this place," Mac says, opening his eyes and gazing into the black hole of the tornado-shaped horn. "I wonder if he even knows it's here."

I imagine having to give Mac and his dad a tour. *Hi, I'm Tegan and I'll be your guide. Come now, let me show you how I ruined your lives.* I adjust my butt so I'm a little farther away from him.

Mac's chin points up as he rests his head back. In his silence I hear the creaks and cracks of our little home trying to stay upright. It might be just the wind outside, but somehow I think not.

The song has been over for some time, and the player is hissing. I stand up and power down the machine for good.

When I turn back, Mac's chin has fallen, his troubled eyes cast down at the powerless phone he's removed from his pocket. He can't totally forget the outside world no matter how hard he tries. "You got a charger here somewhere?" he says.

I tell him where to find it, in the front room plugged into a socket next to the register. He leaves and I exhale. I can't bear to listen to him talk about his dad. I have to find a way to get his mind on something else.

My eyes land on the model of the original Edison laboratory that once resided on this property. It was made with incredible detail: a shingled roof, two chimneys, and curtains in the windows. Not overly exciting on the surface, but it gives me an idea.

"You want to see something, like, really amazing?" I say when Mac returns, struggling to heighten anticipation.

"Obviously," Mac says, as if he's been waiting for me to finally bring the excitement.

"Okay, well, on the tours we give, we always mention that the people who made this model put a tiny phonograph with a tiny record inside the model lab. Supposedly the phonograph actually plays. But I don't know if it's true."

He bends over, hands in his pockets, and peers into the glass enclosure at the miniature world inside.

"I've always wanted to see for myself, but I've never been able to," I say. "Do you want to look now...together?"

Mac seems indifferent.

I smile pathetically. "I like to keep it real boring. We are in a museum after all."

"I'm not bored," Mac says.

He offers it as plain fact, but I take it like a gift. Mac holds his stare. I look away, but not fully. The tops of my eyes watch him.

He turns his focus to our task. "How do we do this?"

"We have to lift the glass top off."

Mac nods, no big thing. There are no handles, so we shove our fingers under the glass through the narrow gap at the bottom.

"Ready?" Mac says.

"I think so."

"One...two...three."

It's lighter than I expect, although I didn't have time to expect anything. It's been that way since I ran out of the house hours ago. Surprise after surprise. I barely have time to process the first one before the next one comes. It's exhilarating, the unpredictability, and terrifying all the same.

I'm doing it again, thinking too much, not paying attention to the direction Mac is steering us. The weight dips, my sudden sweatiness not helping, and my weaker hand fails me—the glass strikes the ground.

Shattered.

The floor is a sea of sparkle. Fragments everywhere. The look of a dream. If only.

I take a single crunchy step. The sound is louder than any speaker Edison ever produced.

"It's okay," Mac says.

I turn, remembering his presence. The crash sent him backward and away. The distance between us feels immense.

"It was an accident," he says.

It makes me laugh. First quietly, then like a lunatic. I laugh with coughing. I laugh with gross spittle. Exhausted, I offer my verdict: "Holy shit."

He squats down and surveys the wreckage. No problem, the hero is here to save the day. He begins to string words together, but it's all nonsense. I barely hear him. I look down at my *special* hand. I shut my eyes and try to stop time, reverse it, end it.

Mac drones on. "Trust me. It'll be all right. It's just glass."

"Expensive glass. You think this place is raking in money? No one comes here."

"Fine, but in the scheme of things, this is just—"

"You don't understand," I say.

As if addressing a child, he asks, "What don't I understand?"

"Me. You don't understand me. You will never understand someone like me."

He shakes his head, smiling that breezy smile. "You're fucking impossible, you know that?"

I want to dip my hands in all the tiny glass crystals and drag them across his jolly cheeks. I walk straight to the bathroom and shut myself inside.

"Really?" Mac says. "You're hiding in the bathroom?"

Yes, I'm hiding in the bathroom with the lights off—for the second time tonight.

"Just say what you want to say already," Mac hollers.

I had planned to ignore him, but now I can't. "This is what I mean. You think you can tell people what to do because...because you're you."

"Who am I?"

I roll my eyes, but Mac can't see me, which only irritates me more. "You don't have to deal with the things I have to deal with."

"You're really going to say that after everything I've told you tonight?"

"Okay, but what about at school?"

"What about it?"

If I have to spell it out for him: "You actually exist. People *like* you."

An overdone laugh. "They don't even know me. All they know is the small part of me I choose to show them."

"I see. So you're fake."

Silence, a little, then a lot. Now some alien resonance through the wall stirs to life, making it hard to hear. Enough time passes that I wonder whether I've missed his response. Or he left.

Maybe that was unfair, the comment about being fake. I keep doing that: saying mean things I don't really mean.

Finally, Mac speaks his mind: "It's simpler that way."

I press my ear to the door.

"It's simpler being what people want me to be."

I was preparing to agree with whatever he said next, because I'm tired of fighting. But I can't agree with him. He's wrong.

"It's not simpler," I say. "It's harder. It takes up so much energy. All that effort, performing, pretending, it's nonstop. What are we doing it for? Why do we care so much what people think of us? Why can't we just say what we want to say? Instead we talk behind each other's backs. That's all everyone does. It's exhausting. It's really exhausting."

The alien drone putters out and allows my embarrassing speech to resonate. The loss of sight heightens my sense of hearing. I don't like the sound of myself.

"Just go already," I tell him, shutting my eyes in the dark.

"No," Mac says.

He's the impossible one here.

"Come out," Mac says. "Let's clean up this mess."

Let's. A contraction of *let* and *us*. It's the second part, the *us*, that gives me the courage I need to do what he's asking. He already had a mess at home tonight that he didn't feel like cleaning up; I wouldn't blame him one bit for walking away from this one. But for some reason he won't.

I open the door and step around him. Inside the utility closet, I find a broom and dust bin. Without making eye contact, I pass the broom to Mac. I slide over a trash can and squat down with the bin in position. He begins to sweep the glass in my direction. When the bin gets heavy, I dump the shards into the trash can.

After enough time has passed, Mac dares to speak. "Just tell them you were cleaning the glass and the thing toppled over."

"I'm not supposed to be here. I wasn't working today." Now I've admitted it.

The trash bin shimmers with diamonds. They clatter and crunch when they strike the bottom of the can.

"I'm the one who's fake," I say.

A tiny admission. Not enough, not even close.

"I think you're the opposite of fake," Mac says.

I stare down at the endless glass, my bin pressed to the floor, awaiting his broom's next delivery.

"You have something in your hair," Mac says.

I rise and face him—in pieces.

He reaches his hand to my head. I ache for him to place his open palm to my cheek, to rest it there until he's made me whole again, or for the first time. But he barely touches me as he picks out a piece of glass. Debris from the crash that must have shot through the air.

Mac holds up the glass between us. I stare through the jagged window back to him.

"I can take the blame," Mac says, tossing the debris in the garbage. "*Everyone* likes me."

He smiles. I find it hard not to smile back. Not every joke makes you laugh. Some just remind you that laughing may still be possible.

Dad,

We started reading Romeo and Juliet in English. All
the years you went on and on about Shakespeare and
now I'm finally reading him.

Love,
Tegan

> Tegan,
>
> Warning: It's a tragedy.
>
> Love,
> Dad

Dad,

I asked Ms. Baker what the poison was that Juliet drank,
and she said it was "incidental." I know if I asked you, even
if you didn't have the answer, you wouldn't tell me it was
"incidental." All that little stuff means something, right?

P.S. I did some digging. People say the poison was
probably nightshade.

Love,
Tegan

Tegan,

Of course the details matter. In my opinion, Ms. Baker is incidental.

Love,
Dad

Dad,

I started reading King Lear. One of your favorites. I don't understand a lot of what I'm reading honestly. But this Regan girl is nasty. I'm a little offended you used to compare me to her.

Love,
Tegan

Tegan,

That was just a joke. I never said I had a good sense of humor. Also, we all have a dark side. There's no denying that.

Love,
Dad

12:54 AM

On my hands and knees, I wipe down the floor with a wet paper towel. Mac drags the heavy trash can to the back door and leaves it there. There's nothing more we can do. A garbage bag wouldn't hold the glass, and the snow outside is too deep to lug it to the shed. I'll be forced to look at my latest mistake for as long as I stay here.

Mac sits next to me on the wooden bench along the wall. We stare into the room.

"I broke something, too," Mac says. "Something I haven't been able to fix."

I look down at the checkered floor, his large sneakers next to my small ones. "Yeah?"

"It was that same night, the night my team and I were at the Cheesecake Factory."

My stomach turns. I don't think I'll ever eat at that restaurant again after tonight.

"I got home after the dinner. I went down to the basement and took my dad's favorite record off the shelf. This album no one's ever heard of. *Meet Muggy Benson.* He would listen to that thing over and over. I slid it out of its sleeve and I dragged my key over it—one long scratch."

It seems no matter what I do or say Mac returns to the subject of his dad. Maybe the only way to take his mind off of it once and for all is to let him get it out of his system.

I ask him, "Was he mad?"

"He was furious. But he never said a word to me. He mostly took it out on my mom. She tried to convince him he scratched it himself and didn't remember. But she knew. She knew it was me. She must have. Because the next time we were alone she told me the story behind it. I knew my dad loved that record, but I never knew why it meant so much to him. It belonged to my grandfather. It was one of the only things my dad had left of his father's."

It's awful. I think of what's left of my dad's things in the house: books, plants, a mason jar full of used wine corks from memorable family meals.

"The thing is, my dad and I have always had a good relationship. He comes to all my games. Never misses one. But he and my brother, they'd bump heads a lot. James could never let anything go. I never understood why he had to be like that."

He drops his elbows to his thighs and props his chin on his clasped hands.

"I've been wondering lately. Maybe my dad and I are only cool because I let him do whatever he wants. Because when James was here, as much as they'd get into it, at least my dad behaved. So my brother leaves and then what? There's no one left to call out his bullshit."

The discomfort of hearing about the inner workings of Mac's household is offset by the gratitude I feel for his trusting me. If he thinks I'm worthy of being let inside, I want to step in.

"Do you ever talk to him about it?" I say. "Tell him what's bothering you?"

"It's complicated."

"Okay, but—"

"I just want to do my thing."

"But he's your dad."

"And? Does that mean he gets to act like an asshole?"

He rises from the bench, too restless to sit. I feel a deep desire to help him find a solution. I'm invested in his story in ways he can't understand.

"When we called 911, you said you thought he was trying to hurt himself. Do you really think he would do that?"

"No," Mac says, pinching the bridge of his nose. "Maybe. I don't know."

"It sounds like your dad has a real problem."

"You think? Shutting himself in a garage with the engine still running? Yeah, I'd say he might have a slight issue."

"What happened after your dad shut the garage? You said you were cleaning up the mailbox."

He holds up his battered hand.

"That's when you smashed the brick," I say, playing his game of charades.

He mimes verification. He's become the silent one now. It's like he's suddenly lost interest in his own story, and *now* he's eager to rush to a new topic.

"Then what did you do?" I say.

He paces around, a tiger in a zoo. My questions are like stones whipped into his enclosure. "What do you want me to say, Tegan?"

"I'm just trying to understand."

"I know what I'm supposed to do. I'm supposed to make sure he gets inside safe, make sure everything's okay. It's what I always do. Why? Why is that on me? No," he says through gnashed teeth. "He wants to get himself killed, let him do it already."

Now his words are stones whipped at *me*. "Don't say that."

"I mean it."

"*I* mean it. Don't say something so stupid."

"You have no idea, Tegan. No offense."

"*You* have no idea." I burst off the bench. "Do you even hear yourself? You act like you have it so hard, like there's nothing you can do. It makes me sick the way you talk about your dad." I'm almost yelling, unable to push down the anger. "My dad, he was just sitting there, alone in his car, at a stoplight, and like that, he's gone. An aneurysm. Out of nowhere. He was in perfect health. If that happened to you, if you *knew* what that felt like, you would do anything you could to save your father, and you wouldn't sound like such a heartless fucking jerk right now."

He stares at me.

I fall back onto the bench. I fold over and bury my face.

The baseboard creaks, struggling to bring warmth back into the room.

"I'm sorry," Mac says.

His tone has softened, the same way everyone's tone softens when the subject of my dad comes up.

"I knew..." Mac says. "I forgot."

It was once common knowledge at school. For weeks after it happened, I was no longer "the girl with the hand"; I was the "dead dad girl." I seriously heard someone call me that. I had a feeling Mac wouldn't remember. Maybe part of me wanted to make him pay for that. Now it's hard to show my face.

"I'm trying to imagine that happening," Mac says.

I wonder for a moment if I've misheard him. I'm so used to people saying the exact opposite—that they *can't* imagine—and it's always bothered me that no one seems willing to try. Mac's willing to go there—wherever I am.

"I guess, with my own dad, I've been kidding myself," Mac says.

The breath he takes is long and weary.

"I tried to stay out of it, what he did tonight. I really tried. But I don't know how. That's why I came to the museum and called 911—or made you do it. It's why I called the house and kept texting him. It's why I made us stop there on our way back."

I peek over. His eyes are lost in the cracks in the floor.

"No matter how hard I try, I can't *not* care," Mac says.

I think of what to say, the exact right statement that can move us past this standstill without diminishing what each of us rightfully feels. He beats me to the talking, using an outer voice that sounds more like an inner one.

"All the things that happened when I was a kid, I thought

they were normal. The yelling. The crying. A birthday party getting canceled. A family trip. The police showing up at our door. My dad disappearing for days on end or becoming super chatty out of nowhere. For the longest time, I thought he just really liked orange juice. I had no idea he was spiking it. I'd have a friend over, and they'd ask why there was a hole in the wall or a tear in the lampshade. I wouldn't know what they were talking about. I didn't even notice that stuff. I was blind to all of it. Until I started seeing other families, the way they were. I'm not like everyone else. Actually, I'm pretty fucked up."

That nasty metamorphosis from normal to freak: I know all about it. How you almost wish you could go back to seeing yourself the way you did when you were younger even though you know full well it's a lie.

"He'll be clean for a long stretch and we'll get used to that version of him. We think the worst is over. But you can't get comfortable. Never. Because it'll happen again. You have to be ready. Unless you're James. He couldn't stand how we'd act like this was all normal. One time he found my dad's stash and broke the bottles on the driveway. It didn't matter. My dad just went out and got more. Now James is gone. What am I supposed to do? My dad's a grown man. If he's not going to deal with all the shit underneath, whatever that is, there's nothing any of us can do."

He inhales forever and exhales even longer.

"Anyway, none of that is an excuse. I just wanted you to know."

I feel horrible for forcing him to justify himself to me. I've already made him feel bad enough about his life by posting that video, and now I'm doing it again. Besides, it's wrong to compare my situation to his. Our fathers couldn't be more different.

But there is one thing Mac and I share: how consumed we are by these men, whether we want to be or not. Mac isn't the only one whose preoccupation borders on obsession.

"Can I tell you something?"

He turns. In his eyes, I feel a vague bond reformed.

"I still send emails to my dad," I say.

He's the first person I've ever told. Saying it to him now feels like a way to take back the secret my mom stole from me.

"We used to email each other a lot. I remember when I got my first account, at nine or ten, I thought it was the coolest thing. My dad would send little notes to my inbox. We kept going like that, back and forth. Whatever we were talking about over breakfast, even if it was something stupid, it would continue over email until he got home at night. The day he died, I had sent him this list I found—the twenty-five best fast-food items. He loved lists, any kind of list, it didn't matter what. He took them really seriously. The list I found had McDonald's fries at the top, and I thought that would bother him, having a side dish be number one. That's the type of thing he'd pick apart. I was curious what he'd say. I kept waiting to hear."

Mac waits now for what *I'm* going to say. I want to say it all—and for him to hear it.

"I kept emailing him after that. I didn't know how to stop. I didn't want to. I used to dream I'd get a response. One day, I decided to make it happen. I broke into his account. It wasn't hard to guess his password. He used the same one for everything. My initials and my birthday. I read his whole inbox. He was still getting mail from people who didn't know he had died and from companies who didn't care. I also looked through his sent mail and read the things he wrote to his friends and colleagues. It was like hearing him talk again. I wanted him to talk again. So I found the messages I sent him, and I replied to them. I made him write back to me."

Whenever I'd see his name in my inbox, for a split second I'd think he was alive again. It feels like that still, even though I know it's just me writing to myself.

Dad,

Were you scared? When it happened, did you know it was happening? It hurts to imagine what you felt. How alone you were. I'm sorry I wasn't there for you.

Love,
Tegan

> Tegan,
>
> It's okay, honey. It was quick. I promise I didn't feel a thing.
>
> Love,
> Dad

Dad,

I look at other people, how they talk. They have no idea how lucky they are. Neel says not to compare. They teach us that in New Beginnings. Don't compare pain. But I can't help it. I keep asking why. Why you? Why did this have to happen to my dad?

Love,
Tegan

Tegan,

There's no answer to why. It's maddening, I know.

Neel seems like a great friend. I'm glad you found him.

Love,
Dad

Dad,

Did you ever wish you had a normal daughter? Did you ever look at me when I was a baby and wish I was like every other baby? Because I look at myself sometimes and I wish that. I would understand if you felt the same way.

Love,
Tegan

Tegan,

You're the only daughter I ever wanted.

Remember when I threatened to kill that old man at Turtle Back Zoo if he didn't stop staring

at you? An old man! That wasn't me, you know
that. I never had a temper. But for you, forget
about it.

Love,
Dad

I remember hearing about it," Mac says. "It was a few years ago, right?"

Three years in March. So yeah, I'm not a fan of March. Or June (Father's Day). But March 9, specifically, is the worst.

"We were in eighth grade," I say.

"Right," Mac says.

"I was at Isla's house. I used to be there a lot. It's one of those houses you never want to leave. We were sitting at the kitchen table, pretending to do math homework, but actually cracking each other up by sending memes back and forth. Isla asked her mom to make us smoothies. Robin, that's her mom's name. She's really cool. Normally she'll drop whatever she's doing if Isla asks her for something. But that day, she was like, 'No, Tegan has to go home.' I remember Isla and I started laughing. We were just in that mood, you know. But Robin was serious. She told me to grab my things. My mom had called her and asked her to drive me home. I texted my mom, just to check in, but she didn't write me back. I thought maybe I was in trouble, but I couldn't think of what for. In the car, Robin was trying to talk to me about school and stuff, but it was weird, she wouldn't even look at me. When we got to my house, I saw my grandparents' car out front. Then my mom answered the door and I saw she was crying."

My mom signed me up for a bereavement group at school, New Beginnings, where I met Neel. He had lost his cousin Avi from a terrible asthma attack. Avi and Neel were like brothers. After it happened, Neel kept having nightmares where he couldn't catch his breath. When I started having nightmares of my own about my dad, I asked Neel when his bad dreams finally stopped. *I'll let you know when they do*, he told me.

Isla and Brooke, meanwhile, keep waiting for me to magically spring back to my former self, a lighter kind of quiet, but I don't think that's how grief works. I can't just flip a switch and be in a great mood and want to hang out all the time. I know they mean well, but only Neel seems to understand that no matter what anyone says or does, the heaviness never fully goes away, even when you're cracking the biggest smile on the outside. Sometimes I don't have the energy to pretend I'm not sad.

Mac asks, "What was your dad like?"

Where to begin? Random memories come to mind.

"He liked puzzles with a million pieces. He was a good doodler. I remember papers with two drawings of the same animal. Two dogs. Two zebras. Two giraffes. His giraffe was always better than my giraffe. I remember his voice sounded much deeper in the morning. I remember I would hold my arm up straight and I would ask him to tickle it and he would. Every time we saw a W.B. Mason truck on the road we'd both say 'yellow truck.' I still say it now. I remember him dancing on the back porch to 'Hey Ya!' He wore glasses, and when I was really little and he came to my room in the middle of the night, if I had a nightmare or something, his face without glasses would frighten me."

I angle toward Mac. "We went tubing—once."

Mac smiles.

"At the top of the hill, before you go down, they give you a choice. They can spin you or not spin you. My dad would get nauseous so easily. He never let my mom drive because he'd get carsick. I don't know how he would have driven around with me with my learner's permit, but anyway. I tell the guy I want to spin, and my dad just gives me the fakest smile ever. He was *so* not into it, but honestly, I didn't even care."

Mac shakes his head. "Ruthless."

"Hey, I was a kid, and I was really excited."

"Go on," Mac says playfully.

"So we go down the hill, spinning like crazy, and when we get to the bottom, he can't"—I start laughing—"he had to *roll* out of the tube."

Mac's dimple shows.

"He stayed there in the snow and people had to walk around him. My mom and I were cracking up. I felt bad, but I couldn't help it. I guess I am pretty ruthless."

"I was just teasing," Mac says.

"Whenever I was in a bad mood or I gave my dad an attitude, instead of calling me Tegan, he'd call me this other name: Regan. I hated when he called me that, even though I didn't get the joke until later. Regan is this really evil character in *King Lear*. One of the king's daughters. Even my dad's jokes were Shakespearean. He was kind of a dork."

I think about him constantly, but he's not usually part of my conversations, not overtly. People don't want to touch the subject, even Isla and Brooke, who knew him well. Neel thinks they're trying to protect me from sadness by not ever mentioning him, but the reality is I'm usually already thinking about him anyway. It feels good to talk about him—my dad. Now that I've started, I don't want to stop.

I look around the museum and more memories arrive.

"He loved this place. Just a few years ago it was really run down and a bunch of people in the community got together to help restore it. He was part of that. At one point, he was here pretty much every weekend. He'd drag me along."

My boss's fondness for my dad is the only reason she granted me a summer internship normally reserved for college students. To make good on that, I tried to read everything I could about Thomas Edison. I figured I owed it to my dad.

"I wonder sometimes when I come here if it was Thomas Edison he was a fan of or just this place. What this place symbolizes. The ideas. He was really into ideas. He knew how powerful they can be."

I think of my "dual touch" idea, the one Neel and I hope to submit to the inventors fair. My dad would have flipped for it. I try to picture his reaction, but his appearance is murky in my mind.

"There's this one invention of Edison's I think about a lot. This machine that lets you communicate with the dead. People called it a ghost machine or spirit box. Edison mentioned it a few times in interviews. He had been working on it a long time. But no one's ever found evidence of one having been built. Plus, no patents were filed for it. I guess he never figured that one out."

I look to the floor, avoiding Mac's eyes. As much joy as it's given me to bring my dad back to life, I feel overwhelmed by all the things I don't remember. I don't remember his smell. I don't remember his laugh, how it sounded. I don't remember his love, how it feels.

Watching videos doesn't help fill in the blanks because he was always the one behind the camera. He was busy shooting my first steps, first haircut, first taste of mashed potatoes. He was busy shooting my worst tantrum and best cartwheel and most drawn-out story. He was busy shooting my birthdays and swim lessons and recitals. He was busy capturing me.

I wish I had captured him back.

How about your dad?" I say, because now I've spilled the beans about mine, and I'm feeling exposed and self-conscious and also guilty that I don't know anything about the poor man I callously threw under the bus. I know he loves music and records but what else? "What does he do for a living?"

"Not sure," Mac says. "Something with computers."

It's both shocking and not that Mac has no clue what his dad does for a living. "Does he like it?"

This, too, gives him trouble. "No. I don't think so."

"My dad loved his job. He was an English professor. At Rutgers, actually."

I had wanted to share this information earlier when Mac mentioned the possibility of going to Rutgers, but I held back. It seems unbelievable now, my hesitation, how fidgety and guarded I felt around him. He's morphed from a unicorn into a human.

"What about your mom?" Mac says.

The casual mention of my mom ruins everything—again. "What about her?"

"I don't know. We keep talking about our fathers. Equal rights, you know."

In this case, screw feminism. "You answer first."

By now he's used to my deflections. He stretches his arms high, the way you do when waking from a deep sleep.

"My mom," Mac says. "She's frustrating."

Now we're talking.

"She complains a lot," Mac says. "But she won't do anything to fix it."

"It?"

"The stuff with my dad. Like, with the mailbox. When she finds out, she'll yell at him, say how we can't have anything nice, all that, but how about actually doing something about it?"

"You mean, like what, getting help for him?"

"Yeah. Rehab, therapy, something. James looked into some kind of retreat. Or else my mom should leave him already if that's what she wants. She *should* want that. They fight all the time. But to just sit there and be helpless..." He's worked himself into a state, an overflow of frustration. "She gets to run off to my aunt's. What about me?"

I guess tonight he decided, finally, that he could leave, too.

The feeling of injustice, I know it well. When my mom started dating Charlie, I was aghast. How dare she move on? Why was I the only one holding on to my dad? It was too big a job to fall solely on me.

"I do feel bad for her," Mac says. "I know she puts up with a lot. She's been out of work, too. She keeps changing careers. If she could find one thing to stick with, maybe she'd be happier."

I can't keep quiet now if I tried. "My mom teaches pre-school. She's a very sweet person. She always sees the bright side. *Always*. It's super annoying."

Mac laughs. "You really are brutal."

"Trust me, it may sound good from afar, but I promise after a while it'll drive you crazy. Especially when you look around and it's obvious that everything is *not* fine. Things are literally falling apart."

These words come with pictures—memories.

I'm up on my feet and heading into the front room. Before Mac can follow, I'm back and carrying a watering can to the bathroom. I fill the can in the sink and carry it to the front room. Mac trails behind. I turn on a small lamp, not the overheads, and climb on a stool. I stand high and water all the plants. Three of them, hanging in a row.

"No one remembers to water them."

I remove a dry brown leaf from the bottom of a pot. I finish watering and sit down on the stool.

"Sorry," I say. "We were talking about my mom."

"Right. What were you saying?"

"No, I mean that's what made me think of the plants."

Mac takes a seat on the other stool. I place the watering can on the counter. A dangling drop falls from the spout and lands on the glass. I flatten the bubble with my thumb.

"When my dad died, no one was taking care of his plants. He had a lot of them."

At the time it felt like everywhere I looked, things were

falling apart. Another school shooting. A post about a tortured dog. A childhood haunt replaced by another cash-and-carry. A tiny rip in my favorite shirt. All I saw and heard—destruction, decay, departure. Things were not fine. I was thirteen.

"My dad used to always be on the phone with this service, this plant hotline. You talk to a real person, not a recording. One day I called the number. This woman—she had the kindest voice—she asked me how she could help. I didn't know what to say to her. So I hung up. I didn't know anything about plants. But I started learning.

"I looked up what kinds of plants my dad had in the house and I called the hotline again. The same woman picked up. Her name was Daphne. I'd describe the problem, whatever it was—the leaves were sagging and yellow, white spots everywhere, growths all over the stems—and Daphne would tell me what to do. More water. Less water. More sunlight. Try feeding it. She had all the answers."

My dad could have looked up the info online, but he preferred to interact with real humans. After talking to Daphne and always having her there to solve my problems, I understand why he liked it so much.

"My dad's plants started coming back to life. It was pretty amazing."

I tried to be as caring and diligent as he was. I really tried.

"But there was one plant I couldn't fix. It kept getting sicker no matter what I did. I couldn't figure out what kind of plant it was. I searched online, but I couldn't find any information. I asked my mom, but she had no idea. I sent a photo to Daphne, but she didn't know what it was, either. I even went to the library. That's what Daphne told me to do. But I couldn't find anything. Not a single mention. It made me so angry—that no one could help."

Mac's chest swells, and in the sigh that follows I feel his empathy.

"My mom kept trying to comfort me, 'It's all right. It's just a plant. It's not important.' But it was important. It was to me. How could she not get that?"

Mac answers what was only superficially a question. "I understand why you'd be upset." He lets this settle before daring to continue. "But if I can push back a little..."

"I'll allow it," I say.

"The other extreme isn't any better. When someone's constantly focusing on the negative. Blowing every little thing out of proportion. It drives you mad in a different way."

I tilt the can, trying to encourage another drop of water to come out. "I guess I can see that."

"Honestly, I don't know that my mom could carry on without my dad. As much as she complains, she'd crumble without him. Your mom sounds pretty tough."

I've always thought of her as oblivious or in denial. Never tough.

"I don't want to make it seem like I hate her," I say, lowering the can. "Of course not. It's just hard to talk to her sometimes. I'm not sure she really gets it. Not like my dad did."

Now, back at home, my mom has access to the whole raw truth.

"She found the emails I wrote to my dad," I say. "That's why I'm here. Why I haven't wanted to go home."

There, I've said it. Mac nods slowly, repeatedly, as if systematically crossing out each of his now incorrect theories about why I might have come to the museum tonight. When finished, he angles his head with puppylike confusion. "Is there something bad in the emails?"

"I don't know. Maybe. That's not the point."

"Okay," Mac says, still processing my big reveal that's maybe not so big after all.

But it *is* big. They were private, those emails between me and him. Or, me and me. I brought him back from the dead, and keeping him alive was a delicate act. The illusion can't continue if I can't forget it's an illusion. She made something special feel laughable, just by her knowing. I can never bring myself to send my dad another email now. Because of her, he's died all over again.

"Those emails weren't meant for her."

He's still confused. "But you sent the emails to him, right?"

"Yeah. So?"

"She probably has access to his account. I mean, I'm sure she needed to get in there at some point. Maybe she's known about the emails the whole time."

Mind. Blown. I've been teleported to one of those copy Earths where everything is almost exactly the same, but not quite. What Mac is saying makes total sense, and yet I can't wrap my head around it.

"Why wouldn't she say anything until now?" I ask.

Mac mulls it over. He's had plenty of experience trying

to solve his own domestic puzzles and seems at ease tackling this one. "Is there something you wrote recently that would alarm her?"

I can't remember the last thing I wrote. It's been a while since I sent my last message. Lately, talking to him hasn't helped me the way it once did.

"So wait," Mac says. "My mom thinks I'm home right now with my dad. Does your mom even know where you are?"

I glare at him.

"Tegan, she's probably freaking out."

I look up at the clock. It's past one in the morning. I've been gone for over eight hours.

It's official: I'm the worst person ever.

10:47 AM

A presence arrived in my bed and forced open my sleepy eyes. Mom crawled in next to me and laid her face in front of mine. I groaned dramatically.

"Oof," she said. "Your breath."

But she didn't seem bothered by it. Bad smells and poor hygiene are her daily reality at school. Her tolerance is mega high.

"You said you wanted to drive today," Mom remembered.

I pulled the blanket over my head. I recently got my learner's permit. I've been driving with Mom mostly on weekends because I'm not comfortable driving at night yet and during the week we can't seem to fit it in before it gets dark.

Our first time out on the road together was rough. We were stopped at a red light and I turned to her. "Am I going to have an aneurysm?"

"No," Mom said emphatically.

"How do you know?"

"Because I won't allow it. You're my everything."

"That's not an answer," I said, waiting for the light to

change. "Can you at least acknowledge that it's a possibility that I *could* have an aneurysm at some point?"

"Fine, it's possible," she conceded. Then almost immediately, she added, "But it's not going to happen."

I felt exasperated by her. But the light turned green and I kept driving, and I'm still driving a month later. I guess she had something to do with that.

Now, in my bed, Mom was telling me to get up. "Come on, kiddo," she said, climbing off the mattress. "The weather is supposed to get bad later."

With my head still under the blanket, I heard the room turn quiet and I wondered whether she'd left. I pulled the covers off my head. She stood at the foot of the bed staring at me.

"What?" I said.

"I'm just watching you," she said.

"That's creepy."

"I can't look at you?"

"Not like that you can't, you weirdo."

I kicked my foot at her through the blanket. It was merely for show. My foot couldn't reach her.

"I have an idea for tonight," she said. "A surprise. It'll be nice."

I sat up. "Why do I doubt that?"

"Because," Mom answered, "you doubt everything I say."

This was clearly a joke, or at least it was clear from her face that it was meant to be a joke, except it couldn't be *just* a joke because of how truthful we both knew it was.

With a playful smile, she said, "So you'll get dressed?"

I got dressed, although I didn't put much effort into it since I didn't anticipate we'd end up stopping at the mall. We went driving because I like to drive and she knows I like it, which is why she dragged me out of bed to do it. I maneuvered through the super-tight Starbucks drive-through so she could treat me to my *first* Frappuccino of the day. And when she grew frustrated by my muteness and remarked that maybe she'd have better luck getting a response out of me if she sent me an email, I didn't even think twice about the comment.

Dad,

I haven't written for a while. I've done something bad.
If you knew what it was, you'd be so disappointed. I
don't know what's wrong with me.

Love,
Tegan

Tegan,

I think it's best that you stop.

Love,
Dad

Dad,

I've been doing everything you taught me not to do.
I've been feeling sorry for myself. I've been bitter and
jealous almost to the point of insanity. I don't want to
feel this way.

Love,
Tegan

Tegan,

You don't have to. You can stop.

Love,
Dad

Dad,

I'm going to stop. I promise. I didn't mean for it to go
on this long. It's just hard. I finally found something
I'm good at.

Love,
Tegan

Tegan,

Please stop. Now I'm begging you.

Love,
Dad

The tiny phonograph," I say, remembering why we decided to remove the glass covering to begin with and, more to the point, hoping to shift our attention away from my mom and the emails.

Mac follows me into the back room. We poke our heads through the doors of the miniature laboratory. It's there, the phonograph, right where my coworkers claimed it would be. I had my doubts.

Our hands are too big to fit through the doors of the model. Mac, with great care, checks the roof to see whether it detaches. It does. He places the roof gingerly on the ground. We now have a clear view of the inside of the lab. There is indeed a tiny record resting on the tiny phonograph. But there's no mechanism to make it spin, let alone produce a sound.

"We had to see for ourselves," Mac says.

He's trying to make me feel better about the glass catastrophe, and I appreciate it, but I don't need cheering up. Even though the tiny phonograph doesn't play, discovering that it actually exists still feels like some kind of miracle.

"Edison invented the phonograph all alone after working on it for months," I say as Mac reattaches the model roof. The wind outside shakes the side of the building, as if threatening to tear off the real roof overhead.

"That's the story we tell," I say. "But in a book I read, I found out what really happened. Edison had a whole team of engineers that helped him. They'd work through the night, take a quick break for midnight lunch—literally what they called it—and get right back at it. They named themselves the Insomnia Squad. One night, in the wee hours, they invented the first phonograph. They did it together. But when Edison wrote about it in his notebook, he didn't mention anyone else on his team. He made it seem like he did it all by himself. And no one doubted him. Why would they? It was his voice on the first ever recording."

It's a simpler story this way and people like a simple story. Mac said so himself earlier. But in this case, the truth seems cooler than the lie.

"Can you imagine the feeling? Sitting there in the middle of the night, exhausted, and together you suddenly create something that no one in the world has ever created?"

"They must have thought they were dreaming," Mac says.

"Yeah."

We share a look. With all the emotional destruction I've caused beyond these walls, to Mac and others, and the physical destruction I've caused right here in this museum, piled up now in the trash can, I can't deny the strange sense that something new is being created tonight between Mac and me. Another kind of late-night invention.

"The Insomnia Squad," Mac says. "I like that."

"Me too."

I smile and he smiles back. It took so long to learn how to speak to him, and now after that initial clumsiness, it's as if I can tell him anything. *Almost* anything. We've revealed so much to each other in such a short span of time and it gives me this powerful urge to go even further, to know all there is to know about him.

"Tell me, Durant."

"Yes, Everly."

"If this tiny phonograph actually worked and it could play anything, what would you want to hear?"

His mouth contorts as he ponders. "I'm not sure."

"Come on. Your dad is a music freak. You're telling me none of that rubbed off on you?"

"I can't think of anything. I like all kinds of stuff."

"Oh, please don't say that. When people say that, it either means they don't listen to music at all, or it's the worst stuff you've ever heard."

He tries to laugh, but it seems forced. "I actually have pretty eclectic taste, believe it or not."

"Great. Name something *eclectic* you listen to."

He shifts awkwardly. I've struck a nerve. "Tell me," I demand.

"What?"

"Just say it."

"It's nothing, it's just—the first thing that comes to mind is not what you'd expect."

Shy Mac is something I've never witnessed before and it's my new favorite thing. I will wait forever for him to come clean and he knows it, too.

"Fine," he says.

"Lay it on me."

"Okay."

"Okay."

"Salsa."

"Salsa?"

"Yeah. Salsa."

I'm not sure how to feel about this.

"I used to take salsa lessons," Mac confesses.

The hugest smile forms on my face.

"Don't laugh," says Shy Mac.

I'm not laughing, really. It's just so adorable, the thought of him.

"I saw an interview with Didé Santos. He's one of the best soccer players in the world. He said he took salsa lessons when he was young. It helped him with his footwork. Good cardio, too."

"Don't try to make it sound better."

"I'm not," Mac says.

"Are you serious? You really took salsa?"

"Why would I lie about something like that?"

"Prove it. Show me."

He walked right into that one. "No," Mac says.

"Yes. Right now."

Shy Mac has become super fidgety. There's no way I'm letting him wiggle out of this. "I'll beg if that's what it takes."

"Beg away," Mac says.

"Please, please, *please*, do some wicked salsa moves for me right now."

"I need *way* more than that."

"I beg of you. I must see this salsa you speak of. I *must*. I *need* it."

Shy Mac seems to be slowly caving. Time to go in for the kill. "I will do *anything* you ask in return," I say.

Now he's beat.

It is with extreme reluctance that he finally says, "I would need the right music."

I rush to the front room. Behind the counter sleeps the museum's prehistoric computer. I awaken the screen and click on the first suitable playlist I find. Salsa music begins to play through speakers in both rooms. I push the volume to its meager limit.

I return to the back room. Mac is seated on the bench as if he thought I might let him off the hook. Sorry. No mercy.

"Whenever you're ready," I say, taunting him.

He shakes his head and says, "I hate you," the way only someone who likes you can say. And then, like the gamesman he is, he sacrifices all and begins to dance. Mac Durant is salsa-ing, for me and me only, and it's goofy and glorious, and I'm giddy and gobsmacked. The music does most of the work. It dances by itself. He ends with a half swing and holds his final position, waiting for my applause.

"Wow," I say, giving it up.

"It's much better with a partner."

My smile vanishes. "Not a chance."

I realize from his sudden change in expression that he wasn't suggesting *me* as a partner. But now that I've mentioned it...

"I'll show you," Mac says.

"No."

"You said you'd do *anything*."

"Not this."

"No one's around."

"You are."

"I'm no one."

"You are the opposite of no one."

He steps to me. "It's only fair."

I'm a terrible negotiator. I promised too much and now I have to pay up.

I retrieve the vodka and take a quick swig. The taste hasn't improved. He grabs the bottle from me and does the same.

We meet on the dance floor. Awkward smile to awkward smile.

He reaches his right arm behind me and grips my back.

"Okay," Mac says. "Now you put your left hand on my back."

My left? He nods. Yes, my left. No mercy.

I wrap my arm around his body, but I don't touch him. I hover my hand over his back.

He raises his left hand and gestures for me to meet it with my right hand. I feel hot. I want to run. I repeat my mantra for the evening: Go with it.

I take his hand. A tingle down my arm. Two untouchables, touching.

"Sorry," I say. "I'm a little sweaty."

"It's okay. Ignore the music. Just take it slow."

I breathe.

"First, you're going to step back with your right foot. Then forward with your left. Forward with your right. That's the first half. Back right, forward left, forward right. Ready?"

"No."

"Here we go. Back, two, three."

I fail to move and he steps on my foot. We both apologize and laugh at ourselves.

"One more time," Mac says. "Slowly. Back...two... three..."

I do it and wait for his approval.

"That was great," Mac says, even though we both know it was objectively awful. "The other half is this. Forward with your left. Back with your right. Back with your left."

He talks me through it. We take it slow.

"You're a natural," Mac says.

A lie. I'll take it.

We settle in. Little by little, we climb up to speed. The music demands that our bodies join it. All the while, Mac counts it out. His chin is held high, but to keep up, I have to stare at my feet. I'm focusing so hard that I don't even realize my left hand is firmly placed on his back until the music changes and a different song begins. This one has a dreadfully slow tempo. A ballad. I look up.

"I clicked on the first playlist I found."

He doesn't let go.

"I'm not slow dancing with you," I say.

It's already happening. We're slow dancing, officially, but holding our salsa pose, a safe distance apart.

His hand slides down my back as we sway. My heartbeats are seismic shakes. I'm weak as an unwatered plant. These are the symptoms of a meltdown, but I'm rising. The feeling takes hold. It makes me light-headed. It makes me dance. *He* does.

He stares into my eyes. It drives me nuts.

"What?" I say.

"Nothing."

"It's never nothing."

"I was just thinking," he says, voice low, barely pushing. "You're the first girl who's ever been inside my house."

My chest squeezes. "Stop."

"It's true," Mac says.

We sway as in a dream.

He gazes at me. "You seemed worthy."

So kind, but it breaks me in half—a sweet thing to say,

a terrible thing to hear. The guilt it brings overruns my heart. I watch the beautiful dream we're suspended in scatter away.

I so badly want to hold on to Mac tighter, but I slip out from his grasp. I can't—I can't do this anymore.

You wish you could say Nightshade quits targeting people because of a change of heart. That you wake up one day and listen to your conscience. It doesn't happen that way.

You're eating lunch, seated at your normal table with Isla and Brooke, plus a few others. Isla is complaining about something, per usual. Brooke is humoring Isla, per usual. You're tuned out, per lately. Or just tuned in to what's going on at other tables. These days, everything you observe is a potential post. There's a beast to feed.

Exiting the cafeteria, there's talk of meeting up after school at the basketball game. No one invites you personally. They just assume you wouldn't come. Which bothers you. Even if it's true, you deserve an invite. To be fair, though, probably no one got a personal invite. It was a vague collective decision. Still.

Afterward, you wait alone for Neel at the archway. You always walk to chemistry together. Today, he barely slows down when he sees you. As if he intends to keep on walking. Moving alongside him now, you inquire about his mood with a simple *Hello?*

I knew it sounded familiar, Neel says.

Okay. And what are we talking about again?

He who shall not be named. Or she, rather.

Sorry. I'm totally lost, you say.

He finally looks at you. *I guess you don't remember complaining to me about Ms. Baker and the whole poison thing. And yet clearly you didn't forget what I said about Ezra.*

You search for the right words. *You mean, what Nightshade posted? Yeah, I read that.*

You read that? Or you wrote it?

You stop still. So does Neel. It's happened—you've been caught.

He leans in. *A Mexican cartel? For real? I said it as a joke, obviously. Why would you post that?*

Staring at the floor. *I don't know.*

So you're not denying it. Nightshade is really you.

You look up with just your eyes. Your chin remains low.

I'm sorry, you say.

People weave around your huddle on their way to class. Neel keeps his voice down when he asks you very earnestly, *What the fuck?*

To that there are many answers. You offer them all. Apologies. Rationalizations. Excuses. Maybe you momentarily forgot where you heard that rumor about Ezra. Or maybe deep down you wanted to be found out.

One thing is certain: Your time as an anonymous troll is officially over. That's it. Nightshade is done. Neel has woken you up from whatever fever dream you were in. Your sense of guilt is immense.

Except...

Except people keep messaging you. They won't stop. They confide in you. Trust you. Share their darkest selves with you. You no longer post their complaints or respond to them, but that doesn't discourage them from writing to you. They don't seem to care. They just want to vent, and you're their best option—a mystery with no face or judgment. You thought you were their voice, but really, you're their ear. You listen to them. You absorb their pain.

A caught B cheating on her; and C feels like the lead role in the school play was given to D because she's the biggest suck-up and not the most deserving; and E is tired of writing papers for ungrateful F; and G is fed up with her own sister, H, who never passes up a chance to belittle her; and J lost her baby before she realized she was pregnant; and when K came out to his parents, they started having him do horse therapy.

You know your classmates better than you've ever known them. Better than they even know one another. Somehow you've found yourself at the very center of everything—the eyes of god.

Every night you try and fail to delete the Nightshade account. As shameful as it is, it's also an achievement. Out of darkness and pain, you created something new that actually matters to people. That wasn't easy to do.

And neither is destroying it.

12:26 PM

I checked my phone while I waited for Neel to come out of the restroom. After driving for coffees, Mom and I stopped at the mall, where Neel and his sister already happened to be (and where they could be found on most Saturdays). I left Mom to shop alone so I could meet up with Neel by the food court.

As I looked down, a pair of basketball sneakers that had never once been used to play basketball appeared. Neel immediately started talking about the project we were supposed to be working on together for the inventors fair.

"I did some research," Neel said. "That glass screen you're touching, it's capacitive. Basically, it conducts electricity every time you put your fingers on it."

I was only half listening, more interested in what was on my phone's screen than how it worked.

"And when the screen responds to how you touch it, that's called haptic feedback. Which is exactly what your idea is about, just with a lot of steps in between. It's definitely possible. Just a matter of the technology. Are you smiling right now because of what I'm saying or something else?"

I was reading a message and didn't realize I was smiling. I lied and told Neel that it was due to his brilliance.

"Tegan."

I looked up.

"What are you doing?"

He said it like he already knew the answer. Like it offended his lighthearted ethos to have to acknowledge something so serious.

"Nothing," I told him, nervous laughter trickling out.

He wasn't buying it.

"Sorry," I said, putting my phone away. "I can't share the details. Patient confidentiality."

His smooth face hardened. "You're not a doctor. You're a gossip junkie."

"It's not gossip. These people are dealing with real stuff, just like us."

"Really? Then why were you smiling?"

I yanked a loose thread from my sweatshirt. Instead of ripping, it pulled indefinitely.

"Come on, Tegan. You said you were going to shut it down."

"I am," I said. "I will."

He looked at me for an uncomfortable amount of time.

"What?" I said.

"You've gone completely fucking crazy."

He walked away, his sneakers squishing.

I followed behind slowly, speaking to his back. "What's your problem?"

He only snorted.

"I'm not doing anything wrong. I don't post anymore. You know that. I'm just…"

He turned. "You're what?"

I averted my eyes. The two of us had been through so much together in just a few short years. Grief and broken Beats and Amma's biryani and the entire Avengers series. He knew all there was to know about me. But this part—the ugliest truth—I didn't know how to discuss.

"I have to go," Neel said.

"Stop it. You don't have to go."

"I do. I have plans."

"With who?"

Now Neel was the one averting his eyes.

"Ezra?" I guessed.

This time his silence was as good as an answer. I couldn't help but notice he was hanging out with Ezra more than usual ever since I'd posted about Ezra on Nightshade. I knew I deserved to be punished for what I'd done. But being abandoned in the middle of such a serious conversation? And for what? I knew what the two of them were meeting up to do.

"Maybe you should try smoking less," I said.

"Maybe you should try smoking *more*," Neel countered. "Might mellow you out a little."

"Oh yeah, Mr. Mellow over here."

"Weed is basically legal, for one."

"Right, I'm sure that would make your parents feel so much better if they found out."

He seemed truly hurt. "Is that a threat?"

"No! Who do you think I am? I'm joking around."

Neel shook his head. "There's a difference between joking around and just being plain mean."

"I'm not trying to be 'mean' to you, dude."

"Fine. Maybe not to me."

I was left to wonder what those last words meant as his sister appeared and forced us to change the subject. I wondered about them in the car with Mom on our way home. I wondered about them alone in my bedroom as daylight faded and the snow began to fall. I wonder about them still.

Standing in front of Mac as the ballad ends, I ask, "Can you do me a favor?"

"Maybe."

"Can you go into the closet?"

I've baffled him for the hundredth time.

"I'm serious. Go into the closet, please."

He's truly at a loss.

I tell him as much as I can. "I have to make a phone call and I don't want you to hear it."

"Can't I just go into the bathroom?"

"No, because you can hear practically everything in that bathroom. The person I'm calling is...my mom."

He looks at me, then at the closet behind him, then back at me.

I make him a promise: "Just for a few minutes."

He heads for the closet. It appears dark and claustrophobic inside. He slides in between the loud furnace and a stepladder. The broom we used to clean the floor is propped up in the corner.

"Smells great in here," Mac says.

I shut the door on him. In the front room, I raise the volume of the new song that's begun and punch in Neel's number on the museum phone.

"Hello?" Neel answers groggily.

Thomas Edison is the one who cemented that particular phone greeting. Alexander Graham Bell preferred *ahoy* as the standardized conversation starter, but Edison's choice won out. If I was calling Neel from my own phone, there would be no need for *hello* or *what's up* or *hey*—he'd just start talking. I'm relieved that he even answered.

"It's me," I say.

"Tegan?"

"Yes."

"Why are you whispering?"

"I have to."

"Where are you?" Neel says, awake now. "Your mom keeps calling. She's really worried. I think she might have called the police."

The police? This has gone way too far. If Mac hadn't arrived tonight, I would have been home hours ago and it wouldn't have come to this.

"I'll call my mom and tell her I'm okay. I will. But first... I just wanted to talk to you."

Our conversation this afternoon might as well have been a year ago. Neel was right to call me out. I just wasn't ready to hear it.

"I'm sorry," I say. "I know you were only trying to help before. You were being a good friend, and I haven't been a good friend back. I've been really shitty, actually."

"It's all good," Neel says, as if he's not quite getting it, and not because it's two in the morning, either. His concerns are elsewhere. "Are you okay?"

"Yes," I say, and then I'm not so sure. "Actually, no. I'm not okay. I don't know what to do."

"About what?"

"About the way I am. Help me. Please. Help me be a better person. How do I do that?"

I hear rustling over the line. I imagine Neel placing a finger to his touch-sensor lamp, sitting up in his too-shiny boxers, removing his mouth guard. Or maybe he just needs time to outsmart the trap he believes I've laid for him.

But I assure him, "I won't be mad. I promise. No matter what you say. Just tell me."

"Stop being a victim," Neel says.

Like yanking a wax strip off my scalp. It's hard to fight the urge to get defensive here. I feel entitled to a rebuttal, but I promised no retribution. I swallow my pride and simply say, "Explain."

"Well," Neel says, sounding taken aback by my civility. "For one thing, all those messages people keep sending you, they're not helping. I'm serious. It's messing with you. You don't see it, but everyone else does, even if they don't actually know what's happening. You've become this closed-off shell around people. Even Isla said something to me about it, and you know I'm not Isla's favorite person. This isn't you, Tegan. It's not how you really are. If you have something to say, you say it. If you disagree, you tell me. You don't back down.

180

You're not scared. You're not shy. Why do you think I started hanging out with Ezra to begin with?"

"Why?"

"Because of you," Neel says. "After Avi died, I guess I couldn't allow myself to have a friend like that. I didn't even realize it until you pointed it out—that basically everyone in my life is a girl."

How quickly reality can combust and reform into a new shape. I feel terrible for guilt-tripping him for spending time with someone other than me. "But why Ezra?"

"Stop. He's a good dude. And we don't just smoke together, by the way."

"Sex?"

That gets a laugh. Suddenly I feel a sense of pride about Neel's friendship with Ezra. That was *my* doing.

"The point is," Neel says, "you're not Nightshade. You're the opposite of that. You need to get that out of your life."

The original meaning behind my alias suddenly becomes obvious again: It's poison.

"Look, Finley Wooten is the worst. Fuck her. That's one person's dumb opinion, and you can't just decide everyone else feels the same way about you, because they don't."

I take a moment to really hear him. Sometimes, as wise as Neel is, I have to ignore his advice—not because I don't agree with it, but because I'm not strong enough to do what's right.

"It's not that easy," I say.

"Obviously," Neel says, and the way he says it drives

home the point that I'm not the only one who feels like a target sometimes. Sometimes, not all the time. Maybe recognizing that distinction is the difference between living like a victim and just living. Neel manages the latter, and maybe I confuse his lack of complaining with his not being affected. If I've learned anything tonight, it's that pain is hiding everywhere.

I don't know why it's taken so long, but finally, in this moment, any lingering satisfaction I've felt from keeping Nightshade open is gone. I'm so ready to be done with it.

"You're right," I say.

"I don't know if I am, but you asked."

I did. And he answered. I'll give him this: He's consistent. Neel has been repeating the same theme to me since the very beginning. He's always tried to get me to be more comfortable in my own skin.

He returns to his original question. "Where are you?"

"I'm at the museum."

"You are? Your mom said Charlie already checked there."

He did? Charlie must have come here when Mac and I were at his house. It feels like there's some divine force that's brought Mac and me together tonight and ensured that we remain that way.

"What are you doing there?" Neel says.

"I'm with someone."

"Who?"

I can't believe I'm saying this. "Mac Durant."

Stunned silence. "I don't get it."

I touch the screen of Mac's phone, still plugged into the wall charger. "I know. I'll explain tomorrow."

I look out the window. The wind is furious, forcing trees into unnatural poses. Snow shoots upward and sideways.

A white SUV passes. Through the chaotic weather, I spot an emblem on the side. The truck drives at an attentive speed and then stops.

"I have to go."

I hang up and crouch low. Poking my head up, I stop the music. I crawl to the back room and join Mac in the closet. I pull the door closed and take cover in the darkness.

"Um," Mac says. "Is there something you want to tell me?"

"Keep your voice down."

"I guess your phone call went well."

"The police are here," I say.

We turn quiet. It's the quiet before the end.

"Are you serious?" Mac says.

"Yes."

"Why didn't you tell me that?"

"I just did."

"Not fast enough. Nowhere near fast enough."

"Please shut up."

"You have to start with that. 'Hey, we have an emergency situation. The police are here.'"

"Please!"

A thump at the door.

"That was the wind," Mac says.

"Are you sure?"

"Sounded like it to me."

We listen, trying to decipher every rustle and murmur.

"Where'd you see them?" Mac says.

"The car drove by and then stopped."

"Did anyone get out of the car?"

"I don't know."

I keep my eyes shut even though I'm blind already.

"You're sure it was a police car?" Mac says.

"It was a truck. An SUV. It was white, so it was hard to see in the snow."

"Shit. Do you think it's about the 911 call we made?" Mac wonders.

"No. I'm pretty sure my mom called them."

"Didn't you just speak to her? I thought you called to tell her you're okay."

The heater hums behind us.

"Tegan," he says, waiting for an answer.

Even in my hiding spot, I can't hide. "I didn't end up calling her. I wrote her an email instead. I saw that she had emailed me, and I emailed her back, saying everything is fine and I'll be home soon."

Lies, lies, lies. I thought I was done telling them. I'm just trying to make things right. Why is that so hard?

"We should go," Mac says with sudden gravity.

"No. Please. Let's stay a little while longer."

He's right. It probably wasn't a police car. I'm being paranoid. Even so, I don't want to face the outside world yet. If there was a way, I'd hold off facing it forever.

"Can we just live in this closet?" I say.

"It's a bit of a downgrade."

His breath nudges me. Our bodies are that close.

"We can start a new society," I say.

"I have some leftover jerky in my pocket," Mac says. "That should keep us alive for a few days if we ration it."

"I don't eat meat."

"You're better off eating meat than Oreos."

"I didn't say I was healthy. I just don't eat meat."

"There might be a few mice in here we can trap."

"Gross," I say. "I wonder if Amazon delivers to closets."

"Amazon *Crime*."

It's so stupid, it makes me laugh. "We can call our new society...Closetopia."

"Closetopia," Mac repeats, testing the sound of it. "Where light never reaches."

"We live in perpetual darkness."

"It does get a little cramped."

"Just a little."

I feel better already. "You know we'll have to procreate at some point."

Stillness. I may have gotten a little carried away by the new optimism flowing through me.

"That was a joke," I say.

His voice blooms in the dark: "Closet life is no place for kids."

"You're right," I say, regaining my senses. "Closetopia should begin and end with us."

"We're enough," Mac says.

I want to kiss him. I thought about it when we were slow dancing and I peered into his eyes, but I wasn't brave enough. It seemed like he was thinking about it, too, how he stared back silently, but maybe I read that wrong. I'm a fine observer but not so good, it turns out, at interpreting. Now we're in the dark, though. Without sight, everything becomes feeling. It overwhelms me, all the feeling. I want to give myself to it, to be the bold and honest Tegan that Neel described, but I need more to go on.

"If we're going to start a society together, I think we need to know everything we can about each other," I say.

"Okay."

"When's your birthday?"

"June fifth. Yours?"

"September twenty-second."

"What would be your last meal?" Mac says.

"Easy. Pasta," I say.

"Same. But what kind?"

"Spaghetti with red sauce."

"For me, it's lasagna," Mac says. "And I want the whole pan to myself."

Dancing with him was beyond intimate, but this is a closer kind of close. When he speaks, his voice rumbles against me.

"Favorite movie," Mac says.

"Dumb question."

"It's not a dumb question."

"If you can choose one favorite movie out of all the movies ever made, then you have no credibility in my book."

"*Fight Club.*"

I roll my eyes. "You're such a boy." And yet he's clearly no fan of the Avengers movies. "If I *have* to answer. I'll go with *Wizard of Oz.*"

"You're lying."

"You'll never know."

I'm not lying.

Mac cracks his knuckles, and the sound gives me mild anxiety.

"Is Mac short for anything?"

He clears his throat. "Macintyre. But nobody calls me that."

"I might have to start. I like it."

"It was my grandfather's name."

There's a joke I've been wanting to make. "I guess you can never use a PC, then."

"Only Apple," Mac says. "It's an unwritten rule."

I'm relieved that we're in the dark, because I'm smiling like a huge dork. So many thrills at once. The thrill of getting to know him and also how much I like what I'm discovering.

"Wait. Is that the same grandfather..." I stop myself.

"Whose record I ruined?" Mac finishes. "Yeah."

I didn't mean to bring up a sore subject. I was just trying to connect the many dots of Mac.

He switches topics. "What do you do outside of school? Like, in your spare time?"

The one activity I can think of is something I can't admit to having done: the throwing of shade. "I like to just, you know, read, watch stuff, listen to *eclectic* music. Lately, I've been kind of antisocial, I guess. I can be a bit of a loner," I say, hoping I don't come off as pitiful as I sound.

"Yeah," Mac says. "Me too."

Really? I'm pretty sure he's the opposite of a loner. Maybe he's got a different understanding of what that word means. "You're friends with everyone."

"I'm *friendly* with everyone."

"Same thing."

"Not really."

Now he's just splitting hairs. "These people you're *friendly* with, do you hang out with them outside of school?"

"Sure. Yeah. Some of them," Mac says.

"Then those are your friends."

He emits a sound, the start of a denial, but he breaks it off to allow for more thought. "I guess I don't have super-close friends. I have some decent ones. Harrison and Glen mainly. And I'm pretty tight with Mike Chang. But no one that I tell everything to. Or even half of everything to. No one that I would go to, you know, in a snowstorm."

Interesting. I ask him, "Why do you think that is?"

"I'm not sure. I guess I feel like they wouldn't understand."

"Understand what?"

"Sometimes I don't feel like smiling or joking around. Then it becomes 'Oh, Mac's in a mood,' or whatever, like I can just snap my fingers. They don't get why I am the way I am."

This sounds extremely familiar. Obviously I'm thinking

of Isla and Brooke. And after talking to Neel, I'm rethinking where part of the blame for our rift may lie. "Maybe that's because you haven't opened up to them. Not fully."

He swallows audibly. "I've tried. I haven't met a lot of people who I connect with like that. Any, really."

I want to ask if this also applies to girls in his life, as in girlfriends, but I delay too long and miss my chance.

"It's my fault probably," Mac says. "A lot of times, when I get invited places, I end up making an excuse. I'd rather be by myself most of the time."

Some of the terms so often attributed to me come to mind: closed off, guarded. I never would have attached those same labels to Mac. Not from afar, anyway. I guess it's like what they say about books and covers. As someone who loves a pretty cover, I always hated that saying—even if it's the truth.

I'm reminded of the initial question that led us here. "If you don't like going out, then what do you do for fun?"

His delay reveals my error. I know what he's going to say before he says it.

"It *was* soccer," Mac says.

Yup. That one hurt.

"I've been playing for so long, I don't even know what to do with myself now," Mac says. "I'd rather not hang at home if I don't have to."

He's so dedicated to soccer that he forced himself to learn salsa to gain a competitive edge. Salsa! Not only did he get robbed of his one true passion, but he also lost his main way of escaping the madness at home—all because of me.

"What if you went back to the team?" I say. "I mean, I understand why you left but..."

I wish I understood less.

"Honestly," Mac says, "people seeing that video, it getting out there, I don't even care. It's not like I didn't hear the rumors about my dad. But the person who took the video, how do you do that to someone? He's supposed to be my friend, my teammate. If you got something to say, come to me, you know?"

"I know," I say, my stomach shredded. How did that video even find its way to me? I'm pretty sure nobody else on Mac's team even goes to our school. Is it possible Nightshade's reputation has spread to other towns? The thought frightens me.

"It seems wrong," I say, "to let one person take away something you love and are good at."

Sage advice. Acquired from my guru.

"I've been thinking of joining an indoor league for the winter," Mac says. "There's one at that new complex on Route 1. It's just been hard lately to get motivated."

It makes me feel a little better that he still might have a way to return to what he loves, and it's reassuring that even *he* feels unmotivated at times. Part of me wants him to start playing soccer again just so I can go watch him.

"I don't know," he says.

I can't tell what this is in reference to, but somehow I totally understand what he means.

He shifts his body, and his hand grazes mine. I pull it away. I wish I were brave enough to leave it there.

"What's your worst trait?" I say, wanting to tear my hand clean off.

The dark quiet reigns as he ponders. "I think I try too hard sometimes to make people happy."

The idea spreads like a weed in my mind. I meant *physical* trait, but he misunderstood.

"What's yours?" Mac says.

My worst personality trait is the complete opposite of his. "I try too hard sometimes to make people unhappy."

He laughs, thinking it's a joke. But my silence soon corrects him, turning him awkwardly still. I hug my knees. I'm as small as I can get.

"Well," Mac says. "Good thing we're in Closetopia. Where there are no consequences."

I breathe too deeply and it smooshes our bodies together. "I love Closetopia."

"Closetopia loves you," Mac says.

He shouldn't use that word. *Love.* It's too dangerous on his lips.

Neel said to not back down. No shyness. No fear.

"I'm curious," I say, scrunching up my face. "Are you... with anyone?"

Time stops. My breath hardens in my lungs. Forehead is pinched so tight I might give myself a stroke.

His answer arrives and plays at magical half speed: "No."

I exhale like a silent ninja.

Now what? What does a person do next?

Be the ninja, Tegan. Be the ninja.

"Why haven't you kissed me yet?" I say.

This ninja is *crazy*.

"Because I'm a little scared of you," Mac says.

I'm set loose, going all in, and too fast—I face-plant into his skull. Instant head throbbing. Concussion-type scenario. A Shakespearean tragedy. "I'm *so* sorry," I say, falling away in disgrace.

But I'm pulled back, collected, and this time I find only softness—lips, his, mine, over and over and over.

The door swings open, our heat escaping in a sultry fog. Despite my deepest desires, we can't stay in the closet forever. We've ignored discomfort for too long and are paying the price. Our necks ache from pretzel-shaped bending. Legs rippling with pins and needles. Hair soaked from thick shared air. We wedge ourselves out one by one.

I glance down the hallway, half expecting to see someone staring into the front window. But there are zero signs of life. Except for the two of us.

I take a seat on the bench. Mac slides onto one of the exhibit tables and I don't have the heart to tell him to get off. He's just a few feet away from me in the back room, but it feels too far. Pressed against him in the dark closet, I felt invincible and free. Now with light and distance between us, I feel small and on display, and it brings doubt. A moment ago I was kissing him and he was kissing me back, and now I can hardly look at him. How do I get back into his arms? It seems such a long way to go.

Mac, meanwhile, swings his dangling legs, relishing the

open space he lacked in Closetopia. He's had his share of girls, I know, so kissing me was probably no big deal. Was it just fun or something more? Was it bad or exceptional? Was it worth doing again?

He inspects a device to his right. "What is this thing?"

I'm grateful to him for saying something, anything, because I don't know where to go from here.

"It's called a hand battery," I say. "One side is silver, the other copper. When you press your hands on it, the needle tells you how much electricity you have in your body."

He places his hands on the device and reads the meter. "Eighty-two. What does that mean?"

"That means you're hot. I mean, your body is." I pretend not to be mortified. Mac may like the sound of my voice, but right now I despise it.

He seems proud of his high number. My reading is down in the sixty range.

"Some people say the higher the electricity in your body, the more prone you are to getting struck by lightning. But I don't think that's true."

"You don't think anything's true," Mac says.

"That's not true."

"There. You just proved my point."

Busted. "I guess I have a hard time believing in what others seem to buy into blindly."

Mac gives me a tough stare. "You have to believe in something."

But how? I've been doubting for as long as I can remember. The hand battery reminds me of one of those memories I keep failing to forget. I decide I'm going to share it because there are no consequences in our new society. Mac promised.

"When I was really young, I made one of those hand-print art thingies at school," I say. "You know, you put your hands in paint and press them against the paper. Obviously, my handprints didn't look like anyone else's."

I lift my stiff leg and lay one sneaker on my thigh. My nail flicks the hard end of my shoelace.

"I brought it home and my parents put it on our fridge. They kept it there for years. I don't know how long it was. I just remember we got a new fridge and they put it on the new fridge, too. Then one day it was gone."

I toss aside the shoelace. I look at him and find him look-ing right back at me.

"What did you do with it?" Mac says.

"How do you know it was me?"

He seems embarrassed that I had to ask—embarrassed for me. It's like no matter what I think I know, I'm always trying to catch up to where he is.

"I tore it up and threw it in the garbage," I say.

He drops his eyes like it was his art I ruined.

"My parents asked me what happened to it. I said I didn't know. They didn't believe me, but they never mentioned it again."

The wind howls as if shedding its own pain.

"I felt terrible. I thought about making them a new one, but it wouldn't have been the same. My hands were so little when I made it."

Mac doesn't say anything, which bothers me at first. But I realize he's prone to his own forms of destruction.

"You said you didn't know that the record you scratched belonged to your grandfather," I say. "How's that possible? Your dad never told you?"

His eyebrows lift as if to acknowledge how improbable it sounds. "When I was young, my dad's parents were always around. They'd come to our house for birthdays, Thanksgiving, Christmas. Then one year they didn't come, and they never came back. No one said anything. There was no explanation." He still can't seem to believe it. "Then, a few years later, I found my dad in the basement crying. First time I ever saw him cry. The only time. I asked my mom what was wrong and she said Grandpa died. We didn't even go to the funeral."

I say the words that I know aren't enough: "I'm sorry."

"I knew it was weird not going to my own grandfather's funeral, but I didn't even realize how weird until recently. It's normal in my family. Aunts, uncles, friends, they disappear from our lives and no one says a word. I can't even wrap my head around all the people my dad has pushed away."

He sighs through a clenched jaw. It turns out Mac is way more of a loner than I realized and for reasons beyond his control. "Why didn't your dad want to go to the funeral?"

"I think he did. He just couldn't bring himself to. They probably got into some stupid fight, he and my grandpa, and they were both too stubborn to let it go. It's sad."

I was thinking the same thing. But I get the sense he means it's more pathetic than heartbreaking.

"I had no idea that the record my dad was always listening to was a family heirloom," Mac says. "I would have liked to know. I might have wanted to listen to it. But it doesn't surprise me one bit that I was never told."

I can't help but hurt for him. He never got to say goodbye to the man he was named after. Then he unknowingly damaged his memory. It was more than a record of music; it was a record of a man.

"Did you ever try to replace it?" I say.

"Yeah," Mac says, fatigued by the subject. "It's impossible to find. Some special import from England or something."

While his dad may have deserved what he got in some way, my parents probably didn't. Even though the art I trashed began as mine, it had become theirs and I took it from them. Worse, I destroyed their precious myth. They *believed* that my hand was normal—better than normal even—and they realized in that moment that I didn't share their belief. I've never been able to buy into the idea. Just a moment ago, in Closetopia, Mac's hands were touching my face, neck, hair. Meanwhile, I held his back with just one hand and tucked the other far out of reach.

It's what I've always done. I hide my hand away. I don't even realize I'm doing it. It's become habit. But there have been times tonight when I either forgot to hide it or couldn't. Like when I was wrapping Mac's hand or doing push-ups or dancing salsa. Was it so terrible to forget about it for a few moments? For me, no. But what about Mac?

197

"Do you think…"

He waits patiently for me to finish.

"Do people think I'm ugly?" I say.

His eyes avoid me and his cheeks seem to redden.

"I really don't know what people think," Mac says, staring at the floor. "I mean, obviously you're really pretty."

Now *my* cheeks seem to redden. "I meant because of my…because I look different."

He lifts his head, understanding what I'm alluding to.

"But what you said…it was really nice," I say.

This idea that I would be *obviously* pretty to Mac is not something I can readily absorb. Neel thinks I'm pretty and he's convinced I know it, too, but that's like your brother saying it.

"I honestly didn't even think about your hand," Mac says. "Maybe it looks different than most, but no, I don't think it's ugly. Or that it makes you ugly. Not for a second."

This, too, is such a nice thing to say, simply uttering the words *your hand* as opposed to referring to *it* or skirting around the issue completely. Still, I'm afraid it's another thing that's too difficult for me to believe.

"Sometimes I just wish I was like everyone else," I say.

"No," Mac says. "You don't want that."

I roll my eyes at his undeniable beauty. "Easy for you to say."

"Come on. Everyone has things they wish they could change about themselves. That's normal."

"Oh yeah? What's your thing?"

Mac points to himself.

"What?" I ask.

"My nose," he says, as if it's obvious.

"What about it?"

"I don't like it. It's too big for my face."

"You're crazy," I say, remembering too late that I don't like to be called that, so I probably shouldn't be a hypocrite.

"It's the way I feel," Mac says. "You can't change my mind."

It's the sort of self-harmony only guys seem capable of. I'd really like some of it for myself.

"Well, I like your nose," I say. "I think it makes you unique."

"I could say the same about your hand," Mac says.

"But you didn't."

"Only because I knew you wouldn't believe me if I did."

Damn, he's good.

He's not the first person to encourage me to see my hand as a kind of gift. There are my parents and Neel, of course. Brooke made me follow a bunch of people online for inspiration, like Bethany Hamilton, who kept surfing even after a shark literally bit off her arm, or Jordan Reeves, who was born without a hand and forearm and invented a prosthetic device that shoots glitter. Even Charlie has tried to drive the point home. *Ray Charles?* he'd say. *Stevie Wonder? What about Django Reinhardt? Django's left hand was mangled and he was one of the best guitarists that ever lived. He created a whole new style that no one before him had ever imagined.*

But can't a hand just be a hand? Because mine came out

different, does that mean I have to, like, want to change the world?

"Charlie is always trying to teach me how to play piano," I say. "He thinks it'll make me look at my hand in a whole new way."

"You mean *the* Charlie Most?"

"The same."

"You still haven't told me who he is."

"He's my mom's boyfriend. He lives with us."

Mac tries to square this new information with the image he already has of Charlie. He brings his legs up and sits with them crossed. "Do you like Charlie Most?"

"Yes. I really like Charlie Most."

"You sound so sad when you say that."

That's just the sound of my guilt.

"Is that his real name?" Mac asks.

I've wondered the same thing. "I think it's a stage name."

"You never asked?"

"No. I think it would insult him. He's an open book with most things. Not his music, though. He likes to keep that side of him really mysterious. I can appreciate that."

Mac squints as if the true mystery here is the one he's looking at. He's right, of course. I thought kissing him might calm the unrest in my belly, but it's only made it worse. My secret was easier to ignore when Mac seemed unreachable. Now that I know what it's like to hold him, to feel his skin against mine, the shame in my gut has become all-consuming. I have to rid myself of this sickness.

"Maybe you should try it," Mac says. "Piano."

"Oh," I say, having already forgotten what we were talking about. "I don't really have an interest."

Mac marvels at my ignorance. "You think I care about listening to old records with my dad? I do it because he's asking and I feel bad saying no. Charlie is just trying to reach out to you. That's all that is."

Dad,

She's so gross. She let Charlie move in with us. They sleep in your bed. Your bed! How could she do this to you? She's such a slut.

But she does harass me a lot less now that he's around. I can hide in my room for hours and no one cares. That's kind of awesome.

Love,
Tegan

Tegan,

Your mother is not a slut. Let's be fair. She waited a long time before she let him move in. That was to protect you. Plus, he was already helping with the mortgage anyway. He should be allowed to live in the house if he's paying for it. And she hasn't forgotten me. She still keeps my pictures up. Even after Charlie moved in.

It's hard to see things from her side, but don't stop trying.

Love,
Dad

Dad,

I tried to hate Charlie. He seemed too good to be
true. But he really is kind and helpful, and nothing
seems to bother him. The only time he gets serious is
when he talks about his music. He says Mom knows
how important it is to him and she doesn't try to
change him.

I used to say no when he offered to drive me places.
Or he'd make me dinner and I'd tell him I wasn't
hungry. But he's a really good cook. I don't know how
to say no to him anymore. Is that wrong? I feel like I'm
doing something bad behind your back.

P.S. I feel terrible about what I said about Mom. I
didn't mean it.

Love,
Tegan

Tegan,

I know you didn't mean what you said. You never
really do.

And there's nothing wrong with liking Charlie. It
would be kind of weird if you didn't. He's a very
likable person.

Love,
Dad

4:24 PM

There was only a hint of daylight in my bedroom when a birdie started singing outside my door. Charlie never knocks. Instead he whistles a mysterious melody, always the same one.

"Come in," I said.

He cracked open the door enough to poke his head in. The big shiny collar of his shirt meant only one thing: show-time. If the weather was as bad as they were predicting, he really shouldn't be out there driving in it.

"You still have to play when there's a snowstorm coming?" I said.

"*Have* to?" Charlie said. "It's not like that. I've been looking forward to this all week. Besides, nobody's canceling a wedding for some snow. People want to get married, they get married."

I often wonder whether Charlie would have asked Mom to marry him already if I wasn't in the equation. I used to think Mom getting remarried would be the end of the world, but that was when the someone she was potentially marrying was a stranger.

"So look," Charlie said. "About this dinner. I happen to know your mom was looking to sit with you tonight. Spend a little time."

"Spend a little time?"

"All I'm saying is, maybe you go downstairs at some point."

I pictured Mom down there now, unpacking all the groceries she had made a special trip for in the snow.

Charlie's thick playing fingers grabbed hold of the doorknob. "See you in the morning."

Before he shut the door, I told him, "She used to cook, you know."

"I've heard."

"She still can. You don't have to do it for her."

Charlie shook his head like I was the silliest thing he had ever seen. "There's a whole lot I do in life that I don't want to. But I promise, cooking for you and your mom isn't one of them."

I told him to leave the door open. In a moment, I'd go downstairs and I'd do as he said: I'd try to spend a little time.

I'm ready for some fresh air," Mac says, jumping off the exhibit table.

It's over, I assume, our time together. We kissed and now he wants to get out of here.

He shoves his palm through his hair, and a clump of it remains upright. I see now that the top of his forehead is sweaty. He's still recovering from the muggy climate of Closetopia.

Mac clarifies. "I kind of want to see inside the tower. That light, the one that never goes out, can you show it to me?"

He doesn't want to leave after all. Not without me, at least.

I get up and crawl back inside his coat. Zipped, buttoned, hooded.

"Yes," I say, excited for the first time at the prospect of parading around the permafrost.

A sign on the back door reads EMERGENCY EXIT ONLY. Mac, wearing the wool hat he briefly lent to the Edison bust, unbolts the door. It doesn't open willingly. The wind pushes against it. Mac heaves it open, and all the heat we stockpiled rushes out. Collected snow topples onto our shoes.

We stand at the threshold. The temperature is deadly. And yet, I feel wildly alive.

We go. Normally the walk would be over in seconds. It's fifty feet tops, but in this weather it requires hefty, tiresome steps. We're not walking but climbing. It looks like a movie I saw about conquering mountains. Men linked by rope. Their lives in one another's hands. We're not tied to each other physically, Mac and I, or even touching, but I feel that I'm hanging on to him for dear life.

Sharp flakes poke at my eyes. I squint and look down. Conditions couldn't be worse. Thick, fierce, relentless. I wonder whether the governor declared the state of emergency he threatened.

The enormous light bulb atop the pointy gray tower guides us. It's the only thing strong enough to laugh at this menacing blast of nature. We climb the slight incline to the terrace and reach the base of the tower. Its tall cement walls, grooved like a Phillips-head screwdriver, shield us. The structure soars nine stories and resembles a rocket ready to shoot into space. Our mission feels intergalactic. I struggle with the key. Mac offers to help, and this time, without resistance, I let him do it for me.

Unlocked, the door flies open and bangs against the wall. We hurry inside and push the door shut. We're spared the wind now but not the cold. It's even more frigid in here. Darker, too.

The room is hardly bigger than a closet. Bare stone and

oppressively empty. Except for a pillar at the center. On top of the pillar is the thing we came for: the Eternal Light.

It isn't much to look at. The illumination is lousy. Faint and unsure. The bulb is cloudy. Like a cheap toy with drained batteries.

"It's really something," Mac says. "Blinding."

"I warned you," I say.

"Yeah, well, I'm trying to make light of it."

"You know, you're the first person to make that joke." My sarcasm wiggles through chattering teeth.

"Okay," Mac says, "so why don't you pretend I'm one of the unfunny guys on one of your tours. What do you want to tell me?"

So many things. I wish I could say them all. My coat swishes as I fold my arms. "They put the bulb here for a reason," I say.

The thick walls dampen the rhythms outside. The cavernous room amplifies my voice.

"Supposedly this is the exact spot where Edison's desk was. It's where he got the ideas for some of his most famous inventions."

The bulb offers a weak flashlight for my campfire tale. I see only the dim outline of Mac.

"I used to believe the story," I say, remembering when my dad first brought me here. "I thought this light held some kind of power. I'd come in here and make a wish."

This hollow place sounds like a church. It inspires confession.

"I used to wish my dad would come back for me. It's stupid, I know."

209

"It's not," Mac says. "I make wishes all the time. I wish my dad would get his shit together. I wish my family could be normal. I know that stuff will never happen but..."

"You don't know that. It could."

He considers it and returns his focus to the cloudy bulb in front of us. "Maybe it only grants our wishes if we touch it."

"Like rubbing a genie's lamp?" I say.

"Exactly," Mac says.

"We're not supposed to touch it."

"We're not supposed to do any of this."

He removes his hand—the unbruised one—from his pocket. He places his palm on the side of the bulb.

I hesitate, but only for a second. It's just a game and I'm playing. I lift my hand, my left hand, and hover it over the opposite side of the light. Then, I let it fall. Our hands touch both sides of the glass—apart but connected.

"Make your wish," he says.

"We should close our eyes first," I say.

He closes his. I stare at him, his eyes closed, so sweet, serene, trusting. He casts his own light, stronger than the one we came here to see. I do the same, shut my eyes. We make our silent wishes. I wish this night would never end. I wish I could take back everything I did and said. I wish my dad would return for me. I wish wishes came true.

We open our eyes. I want to ask what Mac wished for, but then I'd have to reveal my own wishes.

"What happens now?" I say.

"We wait."

"Can we do that back in the museum? I'm freezing."

"Good idea," Mac says.

We walk out of the tower and I lock the door.

Mac stands still in the snow, gazing in the opposite direction. I took too long with the key, it seems, and he's turned into an ice statue.

"Look," Mac says.

I can hear him. I can see him. The wind is still, the snow asleep. It's like god flipped the off switch and bid the world good night. But we're still awake. Aren't we?

I step beside Mac and face the neighborhood. It's one of those trick images your brain can't make sense of right away. My head tilts, my eyes narrow, my mind churns. What am I looking at?

"The lights are out," Mac says.

The image unblurs. The houses across the street are invisible. The streetlights are off. I turn to the museum. I can hardly make it out in the near distance. The front light isn't on. The light is set to a timer and normally stays on through the night, every night, including tonight. Until now.

"What's going on?" I say.

"There must have been a power outage or something," Mac says.

It doesn't make sense. We were gone only a few minutes.

One thing that hasn't changed is the amount of snow on the ground. Probably a foot. Speaking of foots, mine are numb. My socks and shoes were almost dry and now they're wet anew. I can feel the few hairs on my legs squeezing back inside my skin. I'll never get warm again.

"I can't make it back," I say, even though I know I can't

remain out here, either. The storm may be over, but it's left behind an overwhelming impression.

"You want a piggyback ride?" Mac says.

Boys are so weird. Babysitting two of them showed me that. Even a boy as smart as Mac can revert instantly to a dumb animal. That this is somehow cute to me, at least when he does it, is even more confusing.

"Come on," Mac says.

I am not me. I wrap my arms around his shoulders and allow him to take my weight.

He goes full caveman and lugs me through the Ice Age. I've become this primal creature. Everything, suddenly, is that thing I never thought possible—simple. I'm holding on and I'm not heavy, not my heart or mind or body. The doubts that never leave me alone leave me alone. I am the lightest light. I never want to be let down.

His chest expands with each breath, his shoulders firm and strong. I want to find more weight to add so I can crush him. We'll fall together in the snow and be buried in ice for the future to discover. *Look at these two*, archeologists will say. *They died embracing.*

The trip is too short. The calmer weather eases our return journey. He lowers me to the ground.

"I think that counts as my workout for the day," Mac says. The cutest, dumbest animal.

I resort to my own power. I'm weak in the knees. I know now what people mean when they say that. Maybe I'm weak in the eyes, too, because over his shoulder I'm seeing the second mirage of the night.

"Hey, Macintyre."

The name confuses him at first.

I point behind him. "What is that?"

Mac sees it. The top of the tower—the light is on.

He looks at me as if this is part of the standard museum tour. This is a place of science. Whatever is happening now is the opposite of science. It's irrational, illogical, impossible. The power is out everywhere around us. Except here. In this one spot. The tower is lit up. The giant bulb radiates from high above.

"Maybe..." I say.

"Maybe what?"

"I don't know."

He turns to me. "Maybe we're electric."

3:04 AM

Inside, Mac's guess is right: The power is out. It's pitch-dark. Using the available snow light offered by the open door, I locate the candle on the shelf and carry it to the hand crank. Mac meets me there and begins to turn the pencil-sharpener wheel. No electricity needed for this experiment other than what we can generate on our own. Soon the wick ignites and we have fire.

I hold the glass sides of the candle and let it warm my hands. Mac shuts the door to prevent any more of our precious heat from escaping.

I bring the candle to the center of the room and place it on the floor. I sit down next to it, and Mac joins me. We stare at the candle between us.

"My feet are freezing," I say.

We both look up and at the exact same time say, "Cotton." It's hilarious and we're probably the only two people in the world who would find it so.

I kick off my frozen shoes and strip away my wet mismatched socks. I start to caress my feet. I'm cold but smiling.

Mac yanks off his hat and shoves it into his pocket. His hair is a beautiful mess. He lies on his back and stares at the ceiling as if gazing up at stars. His hood serves as a pillow. I want to be where he is. I cross my legs so my feet are tucked under me and I lie back parallel to him. We turn our heads and acknowledge each other's sideways presence. It's like we're sharing the same bed. A very hard bed. At least I wiped down the floor earlier with a paper towel.

Mac reaches for the candle and slides it over so it's no longer between us. It's above our heads now. He raises his right hand off the floor. A shadow animal appears on the ceiling. A bunny. The bunny's face keeps falling apart until Mac finally gets his hands shaped right.

"Hello!" Mac says in a high-pitched bunny voice.

I raise the hand that's closest to the candle. A snail appears on the ceiling.

"No fair," Mac says in his normal voice. "You're not even trying."

One advantage of having a hand like mine.

"What's *your* name?" I say with maximum timbre. This is my snail voice, apparently. It's super deep.

"My name is Bunny," says Bunny, practically squealing.

"You have a very high voice there," says Snail.

"I know," says Bunny. "That's because my owner fixed me. Is your owner mean like mine?"

"No," says Snail. "I'm free to go wherever I please. I just move very...very...slowly."

Inching closer, Bunny says, "Do you want to make out?"

I pause, wondering who should answer, Tegan or Snail.

Out of an abundance of caution, I speak as Snail, saying "Okay," which makes Tegan very jealous—of a shadow animal.

"I have to warn you, though," says Bunny. "I'm an extremely aggressive kisser."

"That sounds perfect," says Snail.

"Here I come," says Bunny. His shadowy shape becomes a tornado of smooching sounds. In seconds, he's finished and resting on the ceiling. "That was amazing."

"Sure was," says Snail.

The. End.

The ceiling goes blank as we lower our tired arms.

"It's not easy to get you to smile," Mac says.

My cheeks hurt from happiness.

You never know someone until you know them. Maybe I still don't *know* Mac, but I know him more tonight than I've ever known him. He used to be invincible, and now I see the flaws in him, but mysteriously, that makes him even more invincible. He still scares me, but in a way that's more thrilling than frightening. My brain is doing somersaults and I'm trying to keep steady, but it's useless, and maybe I don't want to be steady, not in this moment.

I smile at him, with purpose and true joy. He leans in and I meet him halfway. The dark of the closet gave an unreality to our first time, and I do crave the unreal, the liberation of it, but now, seeing clearly who I'm kissing, again and again, is a high I know no match for. Being fully conscious of what's happening, knowing this is a thing I can do, kiss Mac

Durant, openly, repeatedly, is like prolonged astonishment, a feeling of surprise that never goes away.

I pull back, needing a breath. I want to touch his face to make sure it's not fantasy, but the hand that's free is the one I feel less free with. As much as Mac makes me forget myself, some things still seem unforgettable.

I speak in my true voice.

"Earlier tonight, you said most of the time when you're talking to people, you're not even there." I pause, knowing the position I'm putting myself in. "Are you here now?"

He needs only a second. "I am."

The candlelight ripples in his eyes.

"I said something else before." His voice is low and present. "I said it's simpler to pretend. But you were right—it's not simpler."

I stare at his lips as he talks.

"Tonight, when I walked away from my dad in the garage, I made up my mind that I was done. Done acting like everything is fine. I saw you here in the museum, and it was weird, it felt like you saw me back. Honestly, it freaked me out a little. That you could see me. I kept trying to do what I always do, brush things off or whatever, but it's like you wouldn't let me. You wouldn't let me pretend. You're like my brother."

That speech did *not* end up where I expected. I'm humiliated beyond measure. "Wow," I say. "Thanks."

"No," Mac says with a laugh. "Not like that. I mean you remind me of him. The way you can't fake it. It's a good quality. I promise."

The vile burn in my gut spirals up my chest, polluting the pleasure I should be feeling right now.

"All that time we were living under the same roof, James and I, there was something blocking us. But now that he's not around, I don't know, I feel closer to him than I ever did. I feel like I finally understand him." He looks up. "I feel like I understand you."

Me too.

"I feel like you understand me," Mac says.

Me too.

"I've never felt like that before."

Me neither.

"I'm used to, just, feeling alone most of the time."

Yes! But how is it possible? How can someone like him and someone like me share that same feeling? "You said when you saw me at the assembly there was something familiar."

"After what you told me about your dad and what happened, it makes sense. I think I saw you from afar, and I felt some of that."

I thought he was as "normal" as a person could get. As strong and confident as a person could get. That he had more answers than questions, more solutions than problems. The whole time he was more like me than I could ever imagine.

"Were you telling the truth before?" I say. "Am I really the first girl who's ever been in your house?"

"I swear. I've dated girls, and yeah, I just never had them over. Never felt comfortable enough." Mac walks it back. "Not that we're dating, but you know what I mean."

"Yeah," I say. "Obviously."

"Don't say it like that. Why *obviously?*"

"Oh, come on. I'm clearly not like the other girls you've..."

He looks up at the ceiling. "When you asked me point-blank what happened with my hand, I don't know, for the first time, I told the truth. Not all of it, but enough. I realize I don't want to keep this shit inside anymore. I just don't. I think I've been more honest with you tonight than I probably have been with anyone, ever."

The candle trembles, motioning like water. We're deep under the sea, safe in our enchanted home. His perfectly imperfect nose calls out for an Eskimo kiss. He inches closer and a sudden flash illuminates his skin. He stops, pulls back, his eyes searching. Mine search, too. The candle's waves have stilled. We've been wrenched from the ocean. The lights are back on. Power restored.

A loud musical noise emerges from the front room.

"What was that?" Mac says, sitting up.

"Just the computer, I think. It's turning back on."

He rises to his feet. "I'll check."

I wish he wouldn't. What could be more important than what we have going on right here?

I sit up, suddenly aware that I'm lying on the floor by myself. The back room is bright and sterile. The harshness of a dream interrupted. Like when a movie ends and you resurface in the loud and busy lobby. Our movie cut off before it was over. I blow out the candle.

That's one fire put out. Another still rages inside me. I've had enough: I can no longer endure the burn rising up from my core. The sooner I douse it, the sooner Mac and I can

219

move on. What we have is too important to let this stand in our way. It's a misunderstanding, that's all. Compared to what's going on in the present, the past is just that—a misunderstanding. Something otherworldly has happened between us tonight, a forging of souls—seriously, it feels that grand and unfathomable—and now that I'm convinced it's not only me who feels it, that it's not imagined but rather the realest kind of real, I know what I have to do.

Mac made it clear that it's not the video getting leaked that hurt him, but the backstabbing of his teammate, his friend. I refuse to do the same to him. Enough lies. Enough pretending. I'm not fake. Neel knows that. Mac knows that. Mac understands me. He trusts me. I have to trust him back. If I can explain how this all happened, the reasons behind it, he'll get it. It was a mistake. A series of mistakes. We all make them. Mac can appreciate that as well as anyone. How badly our best intentions get mucked up. Our mistakes shouldn't have to define us. Mac knows the true me. He's seen past my hard exterior. He knows my heart. It's time to come out with it—the truth—all of it.

Mac reappears, holding his phone. The screen is lit. His eyes are glued to it. His attention was solely on me. Now it's been hijacked. Damn the electric current that charged that device.

"I can't believe what time it is," Mac says. "Talk about Insomnia Squad. It's after three already. That's insane."

The mention of time hardens the atmosphere around us.

"Should we head home?" Mac says. "I mean, I don't want to but…"

His phone commands his attention. He taps away, typing or searching or commenting, who knows. It's a mystery to me. He is—again. Maybe I've overestimated our connection. He might be this way with every girl, despite what he claims. I have no experience with this scenario and there's a decent chance I'm being delusional. Perhaps in his mind this was a one-night thing and come Monday at school we'll be strangers again.

Here I go, losing all the strength I had just built up. I close my eyes and imagine the voice of my guru: *Be bold. Be brave. Be honest. Be Tegan.*

"I have this sort of random story to tell you," I say.

The insanely late hour doesn't faze me. I'm focused on preserving what we have here and now.

Mac slips his phone away. He walks up to me and steals a kiss. When he pulls back, he makes wacky eyes like a goofball, and I can't help but smile.

"Okay," Mac says. "Tell me."

"Should we sit?" I say, gesturing to the bench.

It's a bad suggestion. It encourages tension. Mac seems on guard suddenly, and that's not what I want. As we sit, I consider reaching out my hand to his, but all my courage is reserved for what I'm about to say. I look into his eyes, golden and inviting.

"We were talking before, a minute ago, really, about pretending. And it made me realize that I've sort of been doing that, a little, with you, pretending."

There's no way out now. But that's okay. There's a way in—honesty.

"Before tonight, I had this idea about you. About people

221

like you. And I thought there was too much separation, maybe, between that type of person, your type of person, and the other type, the ordinary people, the rest of us. I mean, it felt like that. To me. That's what I kept noticing."

"Are you cold? You're shaking."

"Am I? No, I don't feel cold. Not at all," I say, pressing Mac's coat against my body.

"Okay," Mac says, unconvinced. "Go on."

"Yeah, no, this is good. It feels good to say this. I just, yeah, I should slow down maybe. Or speed up? Am I dragging this out? Maybe I'm not saying this right, sorry."

He laughs, relieved, it seems, by the return of my shyness. "For the record, I reject that I'm not an ordinary person."

"Sorry."

"It's okay. Really. Whatever it is."

Yes. It is okay. Being real *is* okay, always. I knew that once, deep in my soul, but I forgot it somehow. I remember now: It's *always* okay to be honest. Even with people who scare you. Especially them.

"I was wrong. I've been wrong about everyone. Even myself. But you, wow, I was as wrong as you can get." I touch his knee with my right hand. "How are you even here? Somehow you are."

He bows his head, trying to remain patient. I pull my hand away.

"I'm pretty sensitive—my friends know that—and maybe I take stuff more personally than I should. But I grew up dealing with certain things, and that puts me on guard sometimes, and I know that's not the best way to go, but I can't help it. Maybe that's my own fault. I'm not trying to say what I did was right, because it's not. I thought it was fair, but only at the beginning. I was upset and I started something and then I stopped. Deep down I always knew it was wrong. But I didn't really know, like, truly, until tonight. Until you came here and made me realize how wrong I've been."

His eyes are hourglasses and I'm running out of sand. "Sorry," Mac says. "I'm not sure what you're trying to say."

"I know, sorry, I'm rambling. I'm going to tell you. I just hope that when I do, you won't forget what happened between us tonight. That would kill me. Like, I'd be—"

"I won't forget," Mac says.

"You promise?" I say, staring into his kind eyes.

"Yes. I promise."

I believe him. I *believe.*

"You know that video of your dad that went around? Well, it was me, actually, who posted that."

He half smirks, thinking it must be a joke. "Okay?" he says, waiting for the punch line.

Some of my courage drains out. I look down at the floor.

"You didn't post the video," Mac says. "Nightshade did."

I nod. He's almost there. Half right.

"I'm sorry," I say. "I didn't know you at the time. Not that it matters. But now, especially now, I would never do that. I would never purposely hurt you." I find his eyes. "You know that, right?"

His forehead folds. "I don't understand."

"So, okay, I started the Nightshade profile on a whim and it just kept going from there. It was a joke, really. Not a joke, sorry, that's not true. It was a way to, just, fight back. To make things—shit, I'm not saying it right. A lot of people, I guess, connected with it, and they started writing me, and I got attached to it. It's like they needed me or something. And that felt good. I know that's horrible to admit, but it's the truth. It felt good."

His smile is gone now.

I cross my arms, hands hidden, pressing my elbows into my gut. This isn't going as I'd planned. How can I begin to explain everything?

I unravel myself as best I can and face him. "I want you to know... it's important that you understand... you are... like, you really... I care about you... a lot."

His jaw tight, he says, "But?"

"There's no *but*. No. It's just—I'm sorry. That's really the main thing I'm trying to say here. I'm sorry. I'm sorry that it happened. I really am. I'll answer any questions you have about it. Anything. I just want you to, like, really understand where I'm coming from."

His eyes wander. His mind searches. He scratches his face.

"I guess it was one of your teammates who sent it to me. I never got the name of the person. Like I said, if I knew you, if I knew your situation, I never would have posted it."

He looks up, and matter-of-factly he says, "Nightshade is you."

I nod.

He turns away. A tangible swerve.

"People started sending me stuff," I explain. "Stuff they

were too scared to say. So I posted it for them. Your team-mate, I guess, was using me to send a message. I'm sorry he did that to you."

"He?" Mac says.

"Well, I know it really upset you, what he did."

He grips his head, stands up. "Oh my god."

The burn inside shoots embers into my throat. The fire spreads. Making it hard to speak. Hard to breathe. And yet, I'm shivering. I can't stop shivering.

Mac paces around the room, determined to put all the fragments together. "So that asshole troll? That Gossip Girl wannabe? That's you?"

"No, that's not me."

"It is you. That's what you're telling me."

"It *was* me. But not anymore." The shivers reach my brain. I have to massage my temples.

He pulls back his hair and holds his head tightly, as if trying to keep his mind from coming apart. "We've been together this whole night. You didn't say anything. You just—"

He grinds his teeth, his disbelief becoming anger. The only right answer here is the truth. That's how you reach Mac. He stated that clearly. It's all he asks of a person. Of me. As hard as it is to get across, it's the only way.

"I thought you were like them," I say.

"Like who?"

"Like everyone else. I didn't think you...that people like you felt pain."

225

He doubles over, exhausted, sick, both.

"I would have told you sooner, but I didn't know if I could trust you," I say. "But that was before. I realize I *can* trust you. Because you know me."

He laughs in a cruel way. "No, I don't."

"Don't say that. Please, don't say that. Yes, you do. You really do."

"I have no idea who the fuck you are," Mac says.

I shut my eyes, keeping the dream alive in my mind. I shake away the shivers, turning my head from side to side. "I'm the same person who's been with you all night."

"How can you say that?" Mac says. "You were lying to me the whole time. Right to my face."

"No."

"Yes."

"No."

"Yes!" Mac says.

"Everything I said to you tonight, *everything*, I meant. You said you came here and that I saw you. I *did* see you. In a way I never have before. And you saw me. Nobody sees me, not all of me. But you did."

He covers his face. His bruised knuckles stare back. "All the things I told you. About me. About my family. You were in my house. You said nothing. You just kept quiet."

Keeping quiet is all I've known. But I'm speaking up now. Doesn't that count for something? Please say it does.

I stand and go to him. "Mac."

My voice used to move him. No longer. "I have to get out of here," he says.

"Don't leave. Please."

He gazes past me at the exit.

"Can you at least look at me?" I say.

He does, but there's no joy in it.

"This isn't what I wanted," I say. "I don't know how it happened."

"You had it backwards. You're the one who's like everyone else."

"What? No, you're misunderstanding."

"I don't think I am. Besides, that's your thing, isn't it? Poor misunderstood Tegan. Nobody understands."

It cuts too deep. My fire ignites. "You're not perfect."

He sighs, as if he finds me pathetic. "I never said I was."

"You basically tried to kill your own father. You just left him there and you made *me* call for help. I can tell everyone what you did. Who you really are."

His eyes light up, ready to detonate, but he pulls back. "You're sick."

He slips around me and walks down the hallway.

I don't have to turn around to see what happens next. The front door beeps. The cold comes in. He goes out.

I follow him to the door. The storm blasts down as he disappears inside it.

He forgot his coat.

5:13 PM

I ran out of the house, my mom calling after. I was already blocks away before I realized I'd forgotten my jacket. It was cold outside, bitter.

The falling flakes felt like debris from my exploded life. I slowed to a walk. What was the point of running when I had nowhere to go? Alone, cold, aimless—I wanted to scream.

When I spotted the moonlike glow of the soaring Edison tower, I realized I'd been heading here all along, to the museum. My body and heart directed me when my mind was fresh out of ideas. I retrieved the key from the old lockbox that had survived the museum's renovation. Under the weak porch light, I fumbled with the lock and wiggled open the door.

The Edison bust recognized me and allowed me to pass. I felt safe. I remembered when my dad first brought me here. *This is it?* I wondered. *It's so small.* Now the snugness was like a hug.

Huddled in a ball on the floor, I reached out to him, my dad, the way I'd been doing for years, with an email, but this

time I didn't send it for real, only in my head. The truth—
even before tonight, I'd given up emailing him. Not because
I'd run out of things to say. He just didn't know what to say
back to me.

I'm not the girl he raised. I don't know who I am anymore.

Dad,

There's nothing you can tell me to make me feel better. What can you possibly say? Aren't you proud of your daughter? You really did create a monster.

Tegan

Dad,

I know you're never coming back, so I'm going to stop wishing. I just wonder if you're the lucky one. Getting to leave like you did. I get jealous of that sometimes.

Tegan

Dad,

I won't bother you anymore. I know you're ashamed of me. I'm sorry it happened like this. I'm really sorry.

Tegan

I look down at my naked feet. Snow fills the space between my toes.

I step back inside the museum, where the shift in light causes brief blindness. I make it to the back room. I can smell him here, I swear, and it brings me to my knees.

I crawl across the floor, bumping into a hard object: the candle. I shove it away. It topples over and tumbles into something valuable.

I crawl more. I crawl until I've reached a dead end. I coil up under the table that Mac once sat on. Where his legs dangled down.

I came to the museum tonight because it was the only place where I could hide. It became a place where I was found.

I shut my eyes and strike the back of my head against the wall. Again, again. A hammer to a nail. Then a sparkle. A swimming, shimmering sparkle. I reach out for it. In my palm, now, a jagged shard of glass. Mac and I missed a piece. I tighten my grip around it and test the sharp edge. It could slice a carrot.

I *am* sick. I tried to prove the opposite to Mac, that the person behind Nightshade is not a psycho, that there were sane reasons behind the madness, that I'm a well-meaning and caring person. But I lost my head again and showed him how truly sick I am.

I shut my eyes and squeeze my hand into a fist.

A list of imperfect things that still function: book with missing cover, person with one kidney, computer without internet, window with cracks, shoes without laces, girl with misshapen hand.

A list of imperfect things that cannot carry on: phone with no charge, chair with three legs, boat with leak, bird with missing wing, girl with broken heart.

Under the table, you squeeze your fist. You'll squeeze until there's nothing left, until it all pours out and fills the cracks in the floor.

You're a pest. Worse than a fly. Another type: bacteria that no one knows is sharing their air. A sickness. Now you're under the microscope—your ugliness blown up.

For a moment, though—for one night, you were more. There was a storm and the sky opened and all turned white and beautiful. Even you. You were beautiful. Truly. You felt it. In your skin. In his eyes. Beating from your chest. You felt it. When you spoke with ease. How time stood still. In the waves of a candle. In a kiss. Your beauty was a bolt. It lit up the dark. It was that real. It could brighten up a house. A night sky. It made colors richer. Songs sweeter. It turned fear into courage. It danced and swayed. Oh, what elegance. What grace. Did you see yourself? You were such a thing. At your most beautiful...

But a dream.

He made a promise. You wanted to believe. How weak, how gullible. Just a pest. A sickness. He was right about you. Not easy. Complex, messy. Brutal.

You're sorry—it changes nothing.

What a beauty, though.

You're sorry—it changes nothing.

A sound…

A figure appearing…

He looks down at the mess you've made.

You're sorry.

His face, kind, relieved, that of a father's.

You're sorry.

His big hands take hold. He drapes you over his shoulder. He takes you away from here.

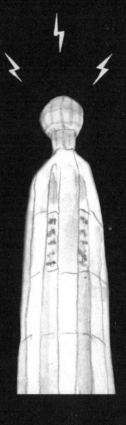

WEEKS LATER

8:23 AM

my eyes open on a different Saturday to a white ceiling. It's a blank screen onto which anything can be projected. I raise my hand and form a shape. With plenty of morning light coming into my bedroom through slanted shades, the conditions aren't right to produce a shadow. I squint my eyes to create a fuzziness around my fingers. Still, the snail doesn't come to life.

I lower my left hand and focus on the right one. Across the palm is a fading red line where the glass dug in. It doesn't hurt anymore. Only to look at.

My phone waits nearby. It urges me to check it and I do. The lock screen is clear of messages. Disappointment, relief. I leave the phone locked.

I throw the covers aside and slide my feet into slippers. I lift the shades to let more light in. The snow is all but gone. A few blackened piles have turned to stone and might never thaw out. What starts out pristine gets made a mess of.

I turn away from the window. The interior view is stained in its own way. This bedroom of mine is too familiar. So much time spent here. The mini disco ball with the forever-tangled chain hanging from the closet doorknob. The leaning tower of books, higher each year, with every lower layer revealing past lives. Wedged inside an empty seltzer bottle— a stress ball looking very stressed. I've stared at these objects for hours on end. When something about the room suddenly changes, it awakens me.

Right now, there's one object that shouldn't be here. It rests flat on my dresser. I walk over and look down. I stare at it, long and hard, feeling wide awake.

The day after the night that changes everything is a Sunday. You waste it entirely in bed. Even if Mom allowed you to leave the house, you wouldn't dare.

The aftermath is worse than the storm itself. Even with doubled-up clothing and covered in blankets, you feel naked. There's only the barest you remaining. Stripped away are the many layers of deceit. Debunked are the various myths you've perpetuated. Fallen is the wall of denial you couldn't see past. There are no more lies worth telling. Nowhere left to hide.

But still you try.

Monday, thankfully, is no school. You would have found a way to stay home even if it weren't a snow day. Normal life, regrettably, resumes on Tuesday. What is normal? Is it chewing handfuls of Charlie's antacids to settle your stomach? Is it lashing out at Neel when he's done nothing to deserve it? Is it arriving late to every class because you'd rather wait for the halls to clear out before showing your face? Has Mac told anyone your secret? How will the masses exact their revenge?

This is what consumes you. But the outcome hardly matters. You're already dead inside. That's what it feels like. Let it be done already. Let the truth be revealed. Let them all hate you the same way he does.

You told him the truth because you thought you could. He made you a promise. You try to hate him the way he hates you. You really put some effort into it. You summon your deepest reserves of venom and you poison his memory with it. This works okay, especially at night, but always when you wake, your thoughts of him are vivid and unharmed, and each one reveals a stunning moment of light and awe.

So there's that.

Obviously, he must be avoided at all costs. You learn his schedule and hallway routes to ensure that the two of you are never in the same place at the same time. Neel serves as additional lookout, texting you Mac's whereabouts while growing increasingly alarmed about this new obsession of yours. You manage to elude Mac for the most part. On Friday, there's a close call. He walks out of the main office as you're passing. He doesn't see you, but his sudden appearance causes a minor panic attack. You wonder why he had to go to the office. Was he called there? Or did he go on his own? As he walks away, his hands dangle at his sides. He doesn't wear a bandage, just a small Band-Aid.

It's not easy, this eternal evasion. Just more pretending, really. The following week, you spot him talking to a group of people. He's all smiles and laughs. It hurts to watch. Is this the real him or a performance? You want him to turn to you and wink, to send you a sign that your time in the museum wasn't a dream. But you realize that no one in real life winks. That night it seemed as if an improbable thing like a wink could really happen. Every tilt of the head and graze of the knee and gleam in the eye seemed equivalent to a wink. The night plays over and over in your head. Every teasing detail. The unharmed memories torture your mind and wring your insides. This life is a kind of death: when the one person you're forbidden to see is the one person who truly sees you.

8:52 AM

I enter the kitchen and find the refrigerator pulled out from the wall. Mom stands before it, arms crossed. Breezy instrumental music bleeds from the house phone lying faceup on the counter.

"What's going on?" I say.

"It just stopped working," Mom says.

Charlie pops his head out from behind the fridge. "Did you break it?"

"No," I answer earnestly, before realizing he's only kidding.

"I've been on hold forever," Mom says, and lowers the volume of the phone. "It's practically brand new, this thing."

"It's almost ten years old," I say, doing some quick math. Three years since Dad died plus at least five more. I was probably around eight when I threw away that hand art my parents had saved.

"Has it been that long?" Mom says, already tired of the subject. "I was just about to wake you up."

"Well. I'm up."

She seems proud that her sixteen-year-old daughter woke herself up for work, and I try not to show that I'm also sort of proud of this small accomplishment.

I open the fridge and peer into the darkness.

"Don't let the cold air out," Mom says. "We still might be able to salvage some of that food."

I shut the door and survey the kitchen. A tray of fresh corn muffins waits on the counter. Charlie says his muffins are organic, but if he's claiming they're healthy, he's delusional. I'm convinced a stick of butter goes into each muffin. They're delicious.

I jiggle a muffin out of its nest and carry it over to the table.

"Do we have any wrapping paper?" I say, crumbs falling from my open mouth.

"For a birthday?" Mom says.

"No. Just something generic."

Charlie pokes his head up, intrigued.

"You need it now?" Mom says.

"Kind of."

She wants to know more, and after all I've put her through she has a right to be curious. I disappeared in the middle of a major storm, and when I finally returned near daybreak, I was covered in blood. That'll unnerve the best of them. But to her credit, Mom resists the urge to pry, perhaps because I've started the day off so responsibly.

"Let me check." Before she leaves, she points to the noisy phone. "If someone picks up, please talk to them."

I hope it doesn't come to that, but if it does, I can manage it. I've spoken under more pressure than this.

I watch Charlie, down on his knees, feeling under the fridge. "Do you know what you're doing back there?"

"No idea," Charlie admits.

"Have you tried unplugging it and plugging it in again?"

"Course I tried that."

Hard to tell whether he's bluffing. I give him the benefit of the doubt.

"Makes no sense," Charlie says. "It was working perfectly last night."

Electricity is like that. It's one of those things we believe in without fully understanding how it works.

"Can I help?" I say.

Charlie hoists his big body up to a standing position. "To hell with it."

He rests in a chair across from me. His forehead glistens with sweat. Hold music loops endlessly from the phone.

I didn't even know how I truly felt about Charlie until that night. Hiding under the table in the museum, letting the glass tear up my hand, I just didn't want to fight anymore.

He arrived like an angel. He carried me to his warm car and drove me home. Not a word between us.

In the driveway, I couldn't get up from the passenger seat, so he lifted me again, this time out of frustration, the compassionate kind, and he delivered me safely to Mom. We embraced and I gazed over her shoulder at Charlie. He watched me like a knight guarding a princess. What he meant to me and what I meant to him—I felt it then.

I feel it now as he wipes his wet brow. I laugh when he pretends to be mean. I adore his lazy spelling in texts. I love that he carries around his MUSICIAN FOR HIRE business cards wherever he goes. I'm disappointed when he forgets to say good night. I miss him when he's gone.

He's even given me my own theme song. I finally asked him what tune he's always whistling outside my door. He told me it's "Girl on Fire" by Alicia Keys.

"Today's the day, huh?" Charlie says, trying not to appear too excited.

"The day for what?" says Mom, returning with her arms full.

I shake my head at Charlie. Mom sees it.

"Excuse me," she says. "No secrets, please."

Charlie wants no part of it. "I'm going to wash up," he says, leaving the table.

Mom watches his awkward exit and turns back to me. Charlie and I took a long drive the other day, and he knows a few things that she doesn't.

"I'll tell you tonight," I say.

Her nerves can't take it. "Tell me now."

"Tonight," I insist, letting her see into my eyes.

She breathes deeply and lets it go. She'll just beat the information out of Charlie if I don't keep my word. But it won't come to that. I'll tell her anything she wants to know, but only after I follow through with my plan.

"I don't have any plain wrapping paper," Mom says, sorting through the items she's dumped on the table. "But I do have these gift bags. Would one of these work?"

On the night of the storm, I warned Mac that he better start appreciating his dad because he could be gone at any moment. I've realized in the time since that I haven't taken my own advice when it comes to my mom. Mac was right: She is tough. She smiles when she wants to cry. She gets out of bed when she needs more sleep. She opens her heart again after it's been torn to pieces. I want some of what she has.

I find a bag that's big enough. "This should be good."

"You're getting crumbs everywhere."

"Sorry," I say, shoving the final bite of muffin into my mouth.

The hold music stops and a woman's voice calls out, "Hello, this is Meredith speaking."

Mom leaps up from her chair and dives for the phone. "I'm here!" she shouts as she fumbles with the receiver.

She takes the phone off speaker. Here's hoping Meredith can save the day.

Mac was right about something else: Mom had known about the emails I was writing Dad for a while. It wasn't her discovery that I was writing them that made her want to talk to me that night; it was learning that I wanted to *stop* writing them.

She had plenty of questions about what she found in those emails. I told her as much as I could. There are still secrets I keep—one very shameful one named after a toxic plant. I don't know whether I'll ever be able to reveal to her how truly low I got. For now, I'm just trying to communicate the best I can.

I take the gift bag and mouth "thanks" to her.

She mouths back, "Text me."

We've been texting each other more than ever. Most of the time it's about nothing—what time I'll be home or where she hid the nail polish remover. But sometimes it's not nothing. Sometimes it's kind of everything.

Do you miss him?

Dad?

Every day.

Every single day.

I just wanted to know.

Some days I think I'm fine and I'm not.

I do something and wonder what he would think.

A restaurant he would have loved. Or a movie.

My standing desk—he'd despise that!

He was definitely a sitter.

Same as me 😉

The worst is watching you grow.

I hate that he can't see that.

I'm sorry. Is that ok to say?

Yes. It's ok.

Thx Mom.

You close the Nightshade account the first chance you get. Even at the very end, people are writing you messages. They still need someone to vent to. It just can't be you anymore.

The morning after the storm you call Neel and give him an attitude because you secretly blame him for how your night with Mac ended. It was his idea that you stop acting the victim and start being daringly honest. But that's before Neel, on that same morning call, asks you if you're crying, and you swear that you're not, but you totally are.

Neel gets you through that first torturous week. The report of how close you and Mac got in just one night makes him a bit jealous, though he'll never admit it.

Okay, I get it already, Neel says after the fiftieth time you've mentioned something Mac said or did.

His dream is to play professionally in Europe, you say, *but he knows he'll be lucky to join a decent college team.*

Neel rolls his eyes. If you were telling Isla and Brooke the same story right now, they wouldn't be trying to change the subject. They'd be begging you to slow down. But they don't know this story. This is one you're not sure you can ever tell them.

For now, Neel has had to get used to the random questions you're suddenly prone to asking: *Do you think I have a nice voice? Is that cotton you're wearing? Should we listen to some salsa?*

You smoke with Neel—once. Because he's hanging out with Ezra and you don't want to be alone, you tag along, and after one measly hit you have a nervous breakdown that takes several hours to overcome. Another night you ask Neel to stay on the phone with you while he plays video games and you read a novel you can't quite focus on. You request his help in wiping the internet of all your posts, and he tells you it's impossible, but he does manage to make them harder to find. Later on, much later than is right, you thank him for being wise to you on the day of the storm and also stupid enough to try to impart his wisdom on a hard-ass like you.

People still don't know who Nightshade was. You keep waiting for the truth to come out. Half of you wants to be outed already. (You have a confessional note saved on your phone, but you can't bring yourself to send it.) The other half wants to lead a life deserving of your good fortune. You're trying to reconnect with the old Tegan. You're also trying to steer clear of social media, but it's hard. You stumble on the latest post by Finley Wooten, the girl who motivated your reign of terror. Finley's family dog just passed and she's devastated. Your first instinct: Her emotion is a put-on. A play for sympathy. But you've learned that your assumptions about people like her have been wrong before. She and you have more in common than you once believed. You've both kissed the same guy.

You create a new account under your real name: Tegan Everly. Your description reads: *Weekend tour guide, sriracha lover, climate concerned, bold AF.*

You go to Finley's post about her dog. You want to leave a comment, but this is the very act that sent you down that odious path. What if leaving a comment creates more trouble for you?

It's a risk you take. You're trying to be better. That means listening more closely to your heart.

You leave the following comment: *So sorry, Finley. I know how bad it feels to lose someone you love.*

Seconds later, Finley likes your comment.

Really? Could it have been that simple all along?

You try it a second time. A third. You tell Erika Reyes that you love when she wears her hair up because it really accentuates her cheekbones, which, you admit, you're totally jealous of. You reveal to Faith Ibori that you feel intense relief every time she asks a question in algebra because you never know what Mr. McKendrick is talking about and you're too embarrassed to ask because you feel like everyone else in the class gets it.

Little by little you try to add kindness to the world to balance out your former wickedness. It becomes your new mission—using your powers of observation for good. Instead of taking people down, you lift them up. It doesn't excuse what you did. Most days the guilt eats away at you. How ugly you became. But you try to remember what you learned: No one is as beautiful as they seem, nor as ugly. Ugly when it's hidden ends up seeming even uglier. Out in the open, though, ugly can look sort of beautiful.

You invite Isla and Brooke to your house for a sleepover, the kind the three of you used to have regularly when you were younger. It's been a while, and you worry there might be some weirdness, but it's as if nothing's changed. Crammed into your bedroom, snacking on veggie straws, you laugh until your stomachs hurt. You really want to tell them about your night with Mac Durant, except you don't know how you'd explain how the night ended or why they've never seen you talk to Mac at school. There's so much more you want to say to them—but not tonight. Tonight you're just soaking up their company.

You keep track of Mac's socials. You can't help it. He hasn't posted since before the storm. You locate the feeds of some of his former teammates. None of them seem to match the person who sent you the video of Mac's dad. Still, studying their accounts gives you an idea. You remember Mac mentioning the possibility of joining an indoor league.

On a Wednesday night, you get yourself to the sports complex on Route 1. You expect to slide unseen onto a bleacher full of spectators, but there are no bleachers and hardly any spectators, save for a few parents standing along a narrow sideline. You turn for the exit, feeling like an idiot, but then you spot him on the field. He's wearing shorts, bare knees exposed, running like a majestic wild feline. It's the picture that matches the thousand words he spoke to you. He's doing what he loves to do, and you're getting to watch him do it. That there are hardly any spectators seems to matter little to Mac and the others. They sprint and dive and fight for the ball as if it's the only thing in the world that means anything. Watching Mac play, focused, panting, sweaty, free, you finally appreciate his passion: It's simple.

There's a pause in play. He stands still in the middle of the field, staring back at you. You're embarrassed to be here but satisfied that he's noticed you. You want him to know you care. But he turns away, and his turning away feels savage, seeing you and then unseeing you. You wait for him to look over again, but he doesn't. You rush out the door.

You want to reach out. To apologize for everything you put him through. You can't text him. You don't have his number. Even if you did, you're not sure you'd be brave enough to use it. A handwritten note might work. But every time you try to put the words down on paper, you fail to capture what you want to say.

Fortunately, you've learned there's more than one way to speak your heart. As painful as it is to rehash every little detail of that night, there's a sense of possibility you draw from the experience. Paying attention brings you a new idea. A way that you might fix the unfixable.

1:35 PM

I send my tour group off to explore the exhibits on their own. We are six in total. Two elderly couples and a frightened woman who gives the impression that she wandered into the Edison Center accidentally and has no idea where she is. They are an attentive group, even the weirdo, and that's all you can ask for.

Working at the museum was just a summer job, but now it's a winter job, too. I'll be "volunteering" here on weekends until the museum can afford to replace the glass display I broke. Which means I'll be here for the rest of my life.

It could have been worse. The museum could have involved the police. Yes, I've worked here in the past, but on the night of the storm (and on previous nights) I was trespassing, which I'm sure is against the law. I also damaged the property, another criminal offense.

I have my dad to thank for the museum going easy on me. My boss, Maggie, wouldn't have a job if it weren't for my dad's efforts to restore this place. It's amazing how he still guides me through life, although he's no longer around.

I don't write to him anymore. But in my head, we're always midconversation.

I call my group back. "Pretty cool, right?" I say, hoping that they've enjoyed their discovery time but also not really caring.

"I'm sure you'll agree, these inventions are impressive," I say. "But Edison's greatest invention of all was Edison."

It's a line that no other tour guide uses. A Tegan Everly original. My group waits for me to explain.

"At one point in time Thomas Edison was probably the most famous person in the world. What's really unbelievable is that this was *before* he produced a working light bulb. *Before* he manufactured any phonographs. Other inventors like Alexander Graham Bell were working on the same projects as Edison and were even further along than he was. So what was the difference between Edison and everyone else?"

A woman in a sari is searching for an answer, but everyone else seems to understand that it's a rhetorical question.

"Edison was a better self-promoter. He was an expert at selling a certain image of himself."

This story used to be my subtle act of rebellion, a way of chipping away at Edison's legend. I thought Edison was a fake. But I was naïve.

Edison never denied that he had tons of failures. Anyone who tries that hard (and he worked until his dying day) is bound to fail. He believed that stumbling was a natural part of the process and that the key to success was to keep going, to keep trying.

Plus, it's important to remember that one person's failure is another person's success. Edison's electric pen was a flop for him, but it led to others inventing the first tattoo pen and also the mimeograph—the precursor to the Xerox machine. It's damn impressive.

So yes, Edison promoted his own achievements, but he also acknowledged his missteps, and I think he should be applauded for that.

"All the celebrities today, they have their brands. Well, Edison basically invented celebrity branding. One more thing to add to his list of credits."

My audience is pleased. They smile politely.

I realized something else recently that has made me ease up on Mr. Edison: People love myths. They love to believe in unbelievable things. These people in front of me don't want to hear anything negative about their hero. They need him. They need his magic.

It's time for the final stop on our tour. I lead my group out the back door and down the path to the memorial tower.

When I came back to work after the storm, I asked Maggie if it was possible that the light on top of the tower would still be able to receive electricity when the whole neighborhood was experiencing a power outage. In other words, was the tower on a separate grid or something? Did it have a dedicated generator?

"I don't believe so," Maggie told me. "I can check with the maintenance guy. Why do you ask?"

"Just curious," I said.

On my tour now, I unlock the door to the tower and instruct my group to gather around the pillar. I'm the last one inside.

"This..." I begin.

It's painful to come back here.

"...is the Eternal Light."

I recite my speech without paying attention to my own words. My mind returns to that night. The way he looked at me. Our hands touching the bulb. I wish I could erase the memory, but I also want to hold on to it forever.

I think also of my dad. I think about the lunch we had at the Rutgers student center when I asked him what my "way in" was and he told me I need to see things. It's not enough for me to hear them. I need to be shown in order to believe.

I end my speech. A frail man with a patchy beard raises his hand.

"Yes?" I say.

"Is it true?" the man asks.

"Is what true?"

"That the light has never gone out?"

People always ask. We're instructed to leave the answer open-ended. To maintain the mystery of the Eternal Light. But I can't help myself. I give the man an answer.

"Yes," I say boldly. "It's true."

Leaving work now.
What's for dinner?

Nothing planned.
We had to buy a new fridge.

How about chicken soup?
If it's not too much work.

I love that idea!
You ok with meat?

Just broth please.

You got it 😊
Charlie has a gig.
It's just you and me.

Sounds perfect.

4:11 PM

Maggie passes me two folded twenties. "A little spending money," she says.

I hold the cash in my scarred palm, feeling thankful and shameful. If Maggie only knew that I allowed our precious Edison bust to get a bloody nose. I give back the money.

"Take it," Maggie says, closing the empty register. "You've been doing a nice job."

Gratitude overrides my shame. I pocket the money.

Work makes the days go faster. It keeps me from thinking too much. I still have an anger in me that I don't know what to do with sometimes. Edison says the trick is to keep going. Keep trying. Keep reinventing. That's what I'm doing.

"See you tomorrow," I say to Maggie.

I zip up my coat and grab my gift bag. As I exit, the door produces that familiar beep. I flip the sign. We're closed.

It's a fifteen-minute walk to where I'm going—the opposite direction from home. It took a lot longer to reach the destination on the night of the storm because of the path taken and the nasty weather. Today the dipping sun shines unobstructed and I'm on the straightest route I can take. I walk with speed, wanting it to be over before I change my mind.

The tan house half concealed by a tree looks different from a few weeks ago—and different from the years before that. Once you step inside a place, it changes how you see it forever. I wonder whether I'm still the only girl Mac has ever invited inside.

At the foot of the driveway is a new mailbox. There are no bricks to be found. The new mailbox is made of plastic.

My pace slows on my way up the driveway. The snowy night had concealed me, but now I'm exposed. I approach the house and the memories flood back. Using his bathroom. The unfinished basement. Lingering in the kitchen. It all happened so fast, I barely had time to pay attention.

At the front porch, my boldness leaves me. I feel like turning back.

Instead, I call my guru. "I'm here," I tell him. "At Mac's. I don't know what to do."

"Just drop it off," Neel says, his mouth full of something crunchy.

"Okay. But where? I didn't think this through."

"Leave it on the porch or something."

The top of the gift bag is wide open. "I'm scared it'll get ruined."

"How about the mailbox?"

I give it a second look. "It's too small."

"Shit," Neel says.

"What?"

"I think these are stale."

"Will you concentrate, please?" I say.

"Sorry," Neel says.

His loud chewing ceases and now I detect another voice in the room. I realize I've been on speaker this whole time.

"Hey, Ezra," I say.

"Hey, Tegan," Ezra answers.

I'm no longer jealous of Neel's relationship with Ezra. He's allowed to have other friends. As long as they're boys.

I guess two gurus are better than one. "Can we *please* focus on me and my problems for a change?"

The boys laugh, maybe a little too much if you ask me.

"Look," Neel says. "I think you're going to have to ring the bell."

"I agree," Ezra says.

"No," I say, glancing around nervously. "I don't want to see him."

"You said he's at work today," Neel says.

"Yeah. I'm almost positive."

"Then don't worry about it."

"But what if his dad answers? I can't face him."

Yes, I owe the man an apology, but that doesn't mean I'll ever be able to look him in the eyes and give it to him.

"Hmm," Neel says. He continues this ambiguous humming seemingly forever.

"Hurry up," I say. "I'm standing on his porch like a damn stalker."

"Just stick it against the door."

A face briefly appears in a downstairs window. "Oh my god. Someone saw me."

"Go," Neel says. "Go!"

"I'm going. I'm going."

I race as casually as physics and self-respect will allow across the Durants' front lawn. When I reach the sidewalk, I stop at the sound of my name. I look up at the house. He's there on the porch.

I mutter to Neel, my lips barely moving, "It's Mac."

"What are you doing?" Neel whispers.

"Just standing here."

"That's not good."

"You think? I'll call you back."

I hang up with Neel and shout an awkward hello over the expanse of the lawn.

Mac starts coming my way. I wait on the sidewalk, petrified, electrified. The last words he uttered to me that night repeat in my ears, the way they have in all the weeks since: *You're sick.* A statement I had been telling myself repeatedly for months before that night, but to hear him say it was far worse. Being with him, I had finally felt un-sick. For the first time in so long, I felt well.

After all the evading and anticipating, Mac lands in front of me in a faded tee, his long naked arms ending in the pockets of his jogger pants. His hair is shorter. The shoes he's wearing look more like slippers, possibly unsuited for outdoor use.

This silent staring is only interrupted when I realize that I'm probably the one who's supposed to talk first.

"I thought you'd be at work," I say.

"Yeah," Mac says. "I quit. It's too much right now."

That he's still willing to divulge anything to me, even this, is a surprise worth embracing. It lifts me off my feet, but I pretend to be grounded.

"I was watching the game," Mac says. "I saw someone out the window."

With a shrug, I say, "Surprise."

I try to read his face. Mostly there's apprehension, and it's earned, I realize, because like a total fool, I'm standing on his sidewalk and I've yet to explain why.

"I wanted to leave this for you," I say.

He looks at the bag pressed tightly to my chest. I release my hold and give him the bag. He peers inside.

"You don't have to open it now," I say.

He pulls out the record, stares at it. First the cover, then the back, then the cover again. There's true wonder on his face, and I'm grateful to be witnessing it, even though I made every effort not to be here when it happened.

"How?" he says, unable to wrap his head around what I just delivered—a piece of his grandfather, Macintyre Durant, the original.

"I happen to work at a museum that knows a thing or two about rare records," I say.

I asked Maggie about the *Meet Muggy Benson* record, and she put me in touch with someone who put me in touch with someone else, and it went on from there. The trail ended, miraculously, in Brooklyn, New York. One physical copy just a car ride away. Charlie drove me.

"How much do I owe you?" Mac says, and it hurts because this isn't supposed to be a business transaction. I don't want anything in return. I only want to lessen his and his family's pain.

"You don't owe me anything," I say.

He looks conflicted. "I can't imagine it was cheap."

"It didn't cost much, actually. I get the impression that nobody cares about this record except your dad."

He smiles. "You're probably right."

"Besides, Charlie lent me the money."

He marvels at it. "*The* Charlie Most?"

"The one and only. He's a sucker for that kind of stuff."

By stuff, Mac assumes I mean music. And I do, partly, but I'm also talking about romance. On our way to the record shop, Charlie started asking questions. *There's this boy*, I told him. That's when he revealed how he found me on the night of the storm. He was driving around hopelessly when he saw a guy walking in the snow.

"I heard you two had a little chat," I say.

Mac nods. "He seems like a really good guy."

"Yeah."

I don't expect Mac to remember, but on the night of the storm, when he heard my parents were no longer together, he said I was lucky. I never thought that word applied to me in any kind of way. But the closer I look at the family I still have, I know I'm wrong about that.

Mac slips the record back into the gift bag. "Well, I appreciate it," he says in that tone that signals the end of a conversation. "My dad will, too."

I guess that's it, then. Earlier today, I have to admit, I had this daydream that Mac would receive my gift and be so blown away by it that he'd come and find me. I'm grateful for this time he's given me, I am, but in the end it's only been a harsh reminder of what I've been missing these past few weeks, and in my life in general. Whatever this is between us, it's so hard to walk away from, even if I'm the only one feeling it.

But I won't be greedy. I did what I set out to do. The video I leaked of his dad was from the same night that Mac went downstairs and scratched the original record. Though I didn't cause the record scratch, I caused other damage, and replacing the record seemed like a way to start repairing everything. I can't change before, but at least I can make a better after.

"Okay," I say, turning to go.

"Wait," Mac says.

I look back.

"Can I walk with you?" Mac says.

I lower my eyes, embarrassed by how much I want this. I fear I'm not worthy of his time, but I accept it shamelessly.

We start walking.

"Who were you talking to before?" Mac says.

"That was Neel."

There's freedom in just coming out with it, the truth. I think back to when Mac asked whether Neel and I were dating and how funny that seemed at the time.

He glances over. "Nice coat."

"I know. I'm pathetic. It's just, it's really warm."

It's *his* coat. I never wear it at school, only on weekends (and sometimes when I'm at home). Meanwhile, he's not wearing a coat—again. Another impromptu trip into the unknown.

"Do you want it back?" I say. "Full disclosure, I've cried all over it."

"That's okay. It's all yours."

It's generous, what he says and how he says it, but still, I feel like a sorry case that he's taken pity on. I can't help it. Self-loathing is my default.

My gut tells me: Put on your hood, keep your head low, zip your mouth shut. My heart fights it: He's walking with you, it means something, make it mean something, don't you dare retreat.

Eyes ahead, I spit it out: "How's he doing? Your dad."

Mac blows warm air into the atmosphere. "He's all right."

It seems that he wants to say more, and I wish he would. I wish he'd open up to me the way he once did.

"Just all right?" I say, welcoming him.

He takes a few silent steps before deciding to speak.

"I had it out with him. I had all these things I needed to say. He went into a hole like he does. But it passed. Ever since he's been okay. I know it won't last. But at least I told him where I stand. That felt good. So thanks."

I give him a look. "Why are you thanking me?"

"That night, the way it happened, it made me realize I don't want to pretend anymore. With anyone."

I know what he means. I wish I'd known a lot sooner.

I stop in the road and turn to the guy who used to be Mac Durant but is now just Mac—or Macintyre to a select

269

few. For one night, he was a person in my life who could be touched and kissed and held, and I was a person who could be touched and kissed and held, and now any interaction short of that feels criminal.

"I'm sorry," I say, struggling to maintain eye contact. "I wish I could take it back. Not that night. But everything before it."

He sighs, for too long. "What you did was really messed up."

"I know."

He looks to the ground. "I kind of hated you."

He kicks a rock against the curb, a move reminiscent of the sport he almost gave up because of me. I'm the tumbling rock against his foot, it feels like.

"But," Mac says, one small word with infinite possibility. "I realized it's not even you I'm mad at. It's just not."

Hearing this is like finding a rising green stem in the soil of a dead plant. You assumed the plant was a goner, but it was under the surface that whole time, refusing to give up.

"That night, I was being real," I say. "I swear to you. As real as I could be. I don't want you to think I'm a terrible person."

He ponders it. "I've seen worse."

A joke, but I'm still not ready to find humor in the situation. "Thank you for not telling anyone," I say. "I mean, I don't know for sure that you didn't tell anyone, but it seems like you didn't. Maybe you did."

"I didn't," Mac says.

"It's okay if you did. You have every right to."

"I didn't."

"Okay."

"Well, just one person," Mac says.

"Oh," I say.

"I'm kidding," he says, trying not to laugh.

I should feel relief, but I don't feel that at all. There's an old pain in my belly. For a split second there, when I believed my secret was out, the pain was finally gone and I experienced something like peace.

"Relax," Mac says.

"I just want it to be over already. Someone has to find out eventually, right?"

"Maybe. But it won't be because of me." His golden eyes were briefly cold, but now they hold warmth again. The promise he made to me that night—maybe he didn't break it after all. He hasn't forgotten.

He asks, "Should we keep walking?"

The answer can only be yes.

We stay on the road, but off to the side.

I'm lucky, I know, to be standing here, a few inches from him, as he swings the bag my mom supplied that contains the gift Charlie obtained, the same gift Neel tried to help me deliver, all these giving hands forming a web of love I'm safely suspended in. I can't help but wonder how Mac fits into this, him and me, if there's any way, any possibility at all that there could be a we or an us. I want to ask where we're going, whether there's a future after now, but I also don't want to ruin a chance to go somewhere unexpected.

"Thanks for coming to my game," Mac says.

It makes me feel good. I didn't think he wanted me there.

"I'm glad you're playing again," I say.

"I'm thinking about rejoining my club team."

"That would be great. I hope you do."

"Yeah," he says, unsure but hopeful. "I want to bring my dad to the museum for a tour."

He's out of his mind. "Not while I'm there, you're not."

"Oh yes," Mac says, relishing my discomfort. "Get ready. We're coming."

Fine. If it means seeing him again, I surrender.

Up ahead, over the houses and trees, the sky is shimmering violet. I wondered whether it would be weird to see Mac again, but it's like we never parted. Talking to him is difficult and easy all at once, and I like that there can be both. Anything less is just people pretending.

"I'm really glad you came in," I say. "That night."

In his smile I see a wink that isn't there, and I believe in my heart that I'm not the only one whose life has been forever changed.

There's just one thing spoiling this moment, and I know full well it'll spoil every good moment in the future unless I finally do something about it.

"Wait," I say, stopping in the road.

I reach into my back pocket for my phone and scroll to the message I've rewritten a dozen times but still haven't posted anywhere. The button that will make it real waits under my hovering thumb. I shut my eyes, summoning the strength. My mind flashes ahead to all the new trouble about to come my way, but it can't compare to the torment I already inflict on myself.

I open my eyes and look at Mac. He waits patiently—for me. If he can see past the ugliest of me to something good and worthy and even beautiful, maybe others eventually can too. Maybe I can.

I press the button. I set myself free.

We walk. I turn off my phone. There will be plenty to deal with—later. I'm scared, but I'm not alone. There's so much light around the two of us. In all the darkness I've made, how can there be so much light? We couldn't see the road that night under all the snow, but now it's laid out before us.

"I went to the inventors fair the other day," Mac says. "I didn't see your project. The touch thing."

I can't believe he went. "We couldn't figure it out in time," I say. "It was too hard."

He steps closer. "You don't need it."

I turn, not understanding. His hand reaches out. I check his eyes, and it's true, he's reaching out for me.

I take in the cold winter air. I take it all in. The storm that came that night blanketed the town, but then it uncovered everything.

I pull my hand out of my pocket, and this time I reach back—with all my ugly.

ACKNOWLEDGMENTS

The Thomas Edison Center is a real place in Edison, New Jersey. Also worth a visit: the Thomas Edison National Historical Park in West Orange, New Jersey.

For more information about limb difference, check out these nonprofits: the Lucky Fin Project and the Amputee Coalition of America.

The team at Little, Brown: Farrin Jacobs—thank you for your faith, taste, and benevolent brutality. Karina Granda. Jen Graham. Emilie Polster. Stefanie Hoffman. Siena Koncsol.

The team at Folio: Jeff Kleinman. John Cusick. Melissa Sarver White. Madeline Froyd. Chiara Panzeri. And at WME: Sylvie Rabineau.

For your singular artwork: Alessandra Olanow.

For sharing your stories and expertise: Claire Chapeau. Brody Marzano. Bennett Madison. Neel Khichi. Beth

Levinson. Mike Emmich. Emily Emmich. Matt Friel. Trupti Patel Doshi. Jen Doktorski. Bethany Mangle.

For believing early and always: Eileen DeNobile (1957–2016). For helping me believe: Collette McGuire.

For my three bright lights in a blackout: Jill, Harper, Lennon.

Thank you.

VAL EMMICH is a *New York Times* bestselling author, singer-songwriter, and actor. His novels include *Dear Evan Hansen: The Novel,* an adaptation of the hit Broadway show, and *The Reminders.*